Charlotte de Rothschild

Addresses to Young Children

Second series

Charlotte de Rothschild

Addresses to Young Children
Second series

ISBN/EAN: 9783337218324

Printed in Europe, USA, Canada, Australia, Japan

Cover: Foto ©Andreas Hilbeck / pixelio.de

More available books at **www.hansebooks.com**

ADDRESSES

TO

YOUNG CHILDREN.

———◆———

𝔖𝔢𝔠𝔬𝔫𝔡 𝔖𝔢𝔯𝔦𝔢𝔰.

———◆———

LONDON :

PRINTED BY WERTHEIMER, LEA AND CO.,

FINSBURY CIRCUS.

—

1867.

PREFACE.

THE first series of Addresses having found favor
with the children for whom they were originally prepared, and having also been indulgently
received by many parents and teachers, the
writer feels encouraged to lay a second series
before the youthful readers and before those
kind friends who take an interest in their
studies.

Like its predecessor, the little book is not intended for publication, but as many copies as
may be desired will be ready for distribution on
application to the printers.

These simple Addresses set forth the principles
which, in the writer's belief, conduce to happiness
through the zealous fulfilment of duty; and it is
earnestly hoped that they may find an echo in
some minds, and help to foster the germs of true
and active benevolence.

CONTENTS.

———◆———

CONTENTS.

I.

SELF-KNOWLEDGE.

My dear children.

Among all the lessons carefully and constantly instilled into your minds at home and abroad,
there is one rule upon which peculiar stress is always
laid — one precept incessantly brought under your
notice, and not only vividly recommended by the
experience of a watchful father, solicitous for your
welfare, or of a tender mother, ever hoping for
your prosperity, and desirous of showing you the
best means of securing it, or by the devoted
teachers, who, in the discharge of their duties,
deem it a paramount obligation to point out the
transcendant necessity of knowledge; but a precept
ardently taught and uniformly handed down by the
greatest sages of all centuries. It comes to you
with the solemn authority of Holy Scripture; it
sounds through ages, dropping, like sweet honey,
from the eloquent lips of inspired philosophers and
kings; it travels to you surrounded by a halo of
unfading glory; it says, with the combined strength
and influence of past eras, " Learn, for knowledge
is power;" it repeats, with the wisdom of modern

B

times, and its myriads of busy tongues, " Learn,
for knowledge is light and warmth :" nor do those
words ever echo, like the wind, through desert air,
or often fall on deaf ears. Far from it; they are
prized like celestial manna, raining down for the
nourishment of exhausted multitudes.

It is pleasant to feel assured, as we do, that
information is now eagerly sought; and that, in
every country, millions of children, and even men
and women, flock to the purest fountains — to the
most invigorating streams of human lore. Yet,
strange to say, there is one kind of knowledge,
and that by far the most precious, which we often
wofully neglect; and this is the more surprising,
as it is knowledge the most easily acquired,
provided we are truthful and persevering in its
pursuit. Such negligence is, therefore, not only
the most guilty and the most extraordinary, because the ignorance, in which we remain plunged,
is entirely voluntary, and completely independent
of outward circumstances and opportunities, but
also and chiefly as the knowledge here alluded to
is far more interesting than the highest branches
of art, the most alluring mysteries of science, and
the most ambitious flights of philosophy. I mean
self-knowledge.

My dear children, you are always able to gain
it, whether in wealth or in poverty — whether in
solitude, or while mixing with the world — whether

surrounded by your loved ones, or eking out
your subsistence among strangers — at all periods
of your life, at every hour of the day, while
floods of sunshine are brightening the time of
labour for you, or while lengthening shadows indicate the approach of night. You need no
lamp in darkness to pursue those important studies
within your soul, nor do any mists by day ever veil
the light of the skies sufficiently to prevent your
seeing clearly into the labyrinths of the heart;
and you require no thread to lead you through
them. Divine goodness provided you with a guide
when it gave you conscience — that faithful companion, inseparable from your inner self, whose
gentle voice is, indeed, so soft and so low, that
the sister, who flings her loving arms around you,
or the mother, who clasps you to her breast,
cannot hear its whispering; yet whose faintest
sound the crash of cannon, the fearful artillery of
heaven, the roaring waves thundering against
basalt rocks, and the whirlwinds howling through
the branches of gigantic trees, are not powerful
enough to drown.

Nor is time ever wanting for a rigorous self-
examination. On opening our eyelids in the
morning, when we awake to the beauties of
nature, and to a renewed enjoyment of the gifts
of Providence, before we shape our feelings and
our hopes into thanksgiving and prayer, let us

turn our delighted looks away for awhile from the
splendours of the rising sun, and from the dew
that sparkles in its earliest rays, and anxiously
endeavour to ascertain whether we are worthy of
the new day that has just dawned upon us; and
whether the blessings of life, and the energies of
body and mind vouchsafed to us, have hitherto
been employed for the advantage of those nearest
and dearest to our affections, as well as for the
good of wider circles — whether we have fulfilled
every duty, developed every gift, exerted every
power, endeavoured boldly to face every fault, and
tried, with all our might, to banish every foe
dangerous to our inward peace. And we may
well be encouraged in the work of daily intro-
spection, when we reflect that it really involves no
egotism, which can lead to baneful results, but
that, on the contrary, it is, perhaps, the only
species of selfishness which we need not fear; for
the more closely we search, the more abundantly
we shall find blemishes that ought to be quickly
removed, failings that should be remedied by the
force of indefatigable perseverance, or good germs,
that have been permitted to lay dormant, instead
of being quickened into useful life, qualities
rusting from inaction, whereas they should have
been fostered and stimulated to lead to the
possession and exercise of every virtue. And
remember, also, that by acquiring self-knowledge

we shall be able to keep our failings in the background, so that they may not become obtrusive and offensive; while a more intimate acquaintance with our powers will encourage us with hopes of success, and, under God's blessing, enable us to attempt the fulfilment of our most important obligations. Depend upon it, my dear children, the craving for every fruit of human lore, the thirsting after the clear waters of truth, the anxiety of exploring heaven and earth for information, are, no doubt, very legitimate emotions, but they should remain subordinate to the feeling that makes us dive for self-knowledge into the deepest recesses of our own hearts.

An eloquent writer has made this important subject unmistakeably evident by many striking illustrations; he has compared our indifference to self-knowledge with the lack of curiosity in one who might for many years have vouchsafed hospitality and the constant shelter of his house to a visitor, without evincing the slightest wish to make his acquaintance, or even to see his features — with the incomprehensible apathy or indolence of a man, who, in possession of the most beautiful collection of pictures, of the finest library of rare books, of the most admirable works of art, has, nevertheless, completely disregarded his own treasures, and never even taken the trouble of looking at them; allowing his choicest volumes to

become mouldy or moth-eaten; and the spider to
hang his obscuring webs over the most glowing
paintings of ancient or modern art—or with the
restless longing of those, who hasten eagerly to distant lands before they have ever thought of becoming acquainted with their own country. And yet, the
writer truly observes, how trifling appears such a
passion for novelty and recreation at a distance
from the domestic hearth, when compared with the
anxious desire of surveying all departments of
knowledge lying far and wide apart, while we are
guilty of the unaccountable folly of neglecting
entirely the regions within our own breast.

And here let me remind you, my dear children,
that long voyages and travels, that studies and
scientific researches are not within every one's
reach; but that bodily or intellectual organisation,
outward circumstances, the want or insufficiency
of pecuniary means, or of remarkable mental
faculties, render the pursuit of art or science often
difficult or impossible; whereas the light of consciousness unfailingly dawns upon us; even the
blind, the deaf, the maimed, the lame, the pa-
ralyzed, can see, hear, walk, and feel in that often
unknown and unvisited land of the heart; and we
want no outward help, not even the assistance of
our senses, nor the activity of our limbs, to guide
us successfully through its mazes. We require
for it much less the aid of costly apparatus, of

telescopes, or observatories; for the power of reflection is a faculty more wondrous by far than any mechanical contrivance; it is unlimited in its action; it is the possession alike of the poor and the rich; and though it may be more completely developed in the highly cultivated, and rendered more penetrating and subtle by practice, yet it is sufficiently strong even in the uneducated and the ignorant, who, though not always able to account for their conclusions, can still view accurately their own thoughts, motives, and impressions, provided they look steadfastly into the workings of their soul.

How strange it appears, that even among those who would feel ashamed of being considered ignorant with regard to general information, and who perhaps eagerly peruse every new work which has any claim to the attention of the public, there are yet to be found many who never pay the slightest regard to self-knowledge, and especially neglect that peculiar root of it, from which the other branches and leaves seem to spring.

It is of real value and importance that every person should be acquainted with the organisation and the laws of his physical nature; the effect of cold and heat upon his system, the inevitable result of sufficient, excessive, or dangerous nourishment; the influence of inhaling pure air, or of breathing a vitiated atmosphere.

With regard to intellectual teaching, whenever it is not simply mechanical, but aims at unfolding all the mental gifts and innate talents, then surely the information should not be given in an empirical way, but should be adapted to the natural tendencies of the mind, so that wit and humour have fair play, that fancy and imagination be guided, enriched, or corrected; that memory be copiously stored; the organs of form, of colour, and language, of time and tune, be duly exercised. But if mere intellectual training ought to repose on an intimate knowledge of the inborn faculties and cravings, how infinitely more momentous is that true and complete acquaintance with our moral nature, upon which depends our temporal as well as our spiritual happiness. The unremitting attention required by our state of health, may, in the years of our infancy or early youth, devolve upon our parents and guardians; later in life, the loving sister, the devoted daughter, may watch over us with fond affection, or the physician may advise us, or prescribe successfully for our ailments; but it is far more difficult for even our most clear-sighted and energetic friends to place a safeguard round our intellectual nature, the defects of which, if overlooked or disregarded by ourselves, may lead us astray into inordinate conceit, or may confirm us in the most obdurate and presumptuous confidence in our own foolish notions and ideas, all drawing us eventually into disappointments and failures. But when our deficiency of self-knowledge regards not our bodily frame, nor our mental qualifications, but relates to the faults of the heart, then, indeed, the peril is great, and there are not words vivid enough to paint it.

It is very true, that we may be so fortunate as to meet with sincere advisers to give us good counsel; but even the most indefatigable guide along the road of life, cannot remove from our path all lacerating thorns, all cutting stones, nor free us from the heavy burden of responsibility. Errors of the soul, far more dangerous than those of the understanding, if unnoticed by ourselves, not merely affect our name or position, but they may make us entirely miserable, hopelessly wretched; while many persons, however unsuccessful in the great world of strife and struggle, may, if all is calm and peaceful within their bosom, find consolation when in communion with themselves.

It has been said, that hypocrisy is the homage almost unwittingly paid by vice to virtue; and there appears to be, not only some peculiar or natural mystery about sin, but also a soft deluding character in its manifestation, as even by the most rigorous examination, moral defects are not so easily ascertained as mental acquirements or shortcomings; for secret faults, singularly enough, often put on the bright garb of virtue.

Thus we are able to mistake silly vanity and sense-less self-worship for love of approbation, that is to say, for the constant aim to win good opinions; the egregious folly of pride for self-respect and dignity; sore-eyed envy for the appreciation of all that is valuable; mean greed and covetous-ness for a laudable wish to improve our worldly circumstances; avarice for thrift and praise-worthy prudence; anger, and even hatred and revengeful sentiments, for a high spirit of independ-ence, for a discriminating knowledge of right and wrong, for fine and delicate feeling as contrasted with indifference and negligence. Most justly does the Psalmist say, "Who can understand his errors; cleanse Thou me from secret faults!" The ugliness of sin may, probably, explain its self-concealing tendency; one of its features, how-ever, that has been frequently pointed out, is undeniable, namely, that it becomes en-tirely evident only when strongly repulsed;— quietly and passively it is never given up.

It seems like the turbulent stream, whose rapidity is not noticed, until the boat, on its wildly-dashing waters, strives to withstand the mad current that would sweep it along; or similar to the billows, whose height and strength remain unknown, until broken by hard

or towering reefs; or, it may be compared to the
blast, which, almost noiseless when flying over
broad wastes or moors, becomes alarming when
it howls round lofty masts, or wails and moans at
doors and windows, closed and barred against its
fury.

Sin often makes us feel ashamed of knowing ourselves. Some of us may, perhaps, have suspected, or
seen, one little frightful corner, and then shrunk
from the pain of unveiling to their mind's eye, the
whole humiliating picture of their faults and
failings. Yet such willing blindness relates
chiefly to our inward being. With regard to
outward circumstances, we should consider our
apathy unpardonable, and almost amounting to
insanity, if, when threatened with danger to life
or fortune, with the horrors of shipwreck or fire,
with death from the fang of serpents, or the rage
of savage animals, or with ruin from the effects
of reckless speculation, we did not endeavour to
escape from peril; or if, when sickness is approaching, we awaited death, either without
calling in a physician, or without heeding his
advice and prescriptions.

Yet, rare and startling, and almost incredible,
as such utter indifference and neglect may seem
to be in the general affairs and incidents of life;
in matters of spiritual interest, there are, I am
afraid, too many persons, who but seldom en-

deavour to penetrate into the chambers of their breast. It is, however, impossible to pass through life, without experiencing sickness and sorrow; and, under such painful visitations, conscience, long dumb or silenced, speaks reproachfully to the most careless ear; harassing anxiety tortures the soul, and remorseful pangs trouble even the most heedless and the most obdurate.

During many years, perhaps under the broad disc of trifling annoyances, fleeting amusements, and frivolous pleasures, our true nature lies dormant and torpid; but death, which carries off our most dearly-loved friends and companions, or threatens their existence as well as our own brief tenure of life, awakens, with dread and suffering, the somnolent soul, and leaves it trembling in its helplessness, to face the unknown power.

Again: self-ignorance is explained by the often slow and imperceptible steps by which sinful habits are contracted. The changes which thus take place in us, have, therefore, been justly compared to those that occur in the outward world, when one season merges by degrees into the other; and we are led, by the gentlest transitions from blooming spring, with its myriads of sweetly-scented flowers, to glowing summer and its golden harvests, to fruitful autumn and its generous gifts, imperceptibly on to dreary winter, so cold and so bare, so leafless and so colourless. Thus childhood, with its sunny looks and ruby lips, its laughter-loving voice, that knows no care, gives way to blushing girlhood, with its bright dreams and fond hopes; while that again disappears before womanhood, with its load of duties and responsibilities, until hoary old age, often with frowns and furrows, and surrounded by regrets and self-reproaches, brings us, unawares, to life's decline.

Similar alterations take place, unobserved or unheeded, in our character. Frequently, as in our external form, the gradual growth and development of faults in our inward nature, while becoming disagreeably apparent to others, remain unnoticed by us; we omit to question conscience, that mirror of the soul; we close our eyes and ears, and let the work of internal havoc go on silently and invisibly: for, alas! as the character decays and becomes defaced, there is a parallel decline of the principle by which we judge of it; the power which perceives sin, partakes of the general injury, and does not remain stationary.

You will understand me better, if I illustrate my meaning by reminding you that when palsy becomes confirmed, the unfortunate sufferers lose, not merely the faculty of directing their movements, but also the bodily power of sensation and perception; for instance, they do not feel the difference between ice and glowing coals, between the most rugged stone and the softest swan's down, between the touch of a rose-leaf or the impression of burning caustic. The morally indifferent appear like patients in a deep magnetic trance, who are said to bear the infliction of pins and needles, thrust into their flesh, without shrinking or even murmuring. But they do wake and shudder at the injury inflicted during their sleep. So does our moral nature wake, when sorrows and calamities rouse us; it wakes and trembles at the slow fever, which, like a painless cancer, deadened by powerful opiates, has devoured our best qualities, and burnt and drunk our purest life-blood away.

Nor must you suppose, my dear children, that self-ignorance can be an excuse for wrong-doing; in such a case, guilt and danger walk hand-in-hand; having destroyed the torch that would have guided us, we are, of course, liable to fall in the dark, having willingly closed our ears to the powerfully warning voice within, we are bereft of our most precious treasures of thought and feeling. Well-defined dangers may be avoided or overcome; but who can wage war against unseen traps and snares?

Therefore, my dear children, look stedfastly, carefully and perseveringly into the depths of your hearts; hearken attentively and eagerly to the admonitions of conscience; think that you have to maintain the purity of your souls before God, and thank Him humbly and lovingly for all His favours and blessings. But do not, for a single moment, forget, that self-knowledge was never intended by the Divine Creator to lead you to egotism; that it is, on the contrary, intended as the best and surest means of guiding you to the fulfilment of all your duties towards your fellow-men. For had you been designed to live quite alone, on the airy heights of mountain-crests, or, below, in the most fruitful valley of any desert island, self-revelation would scarcely be requisite; you would certainly have the sacred obligation of gratitude to your Almighty Maker and Preserver, and of devout appreciation of all the gifts of His goodness; but, in your total isolation, your breast could harbour neither covetousness nor pride, neither anger, nor malice, nor hatred, nor resentment, nor violence; nor would you have any scope for generosity and charity; for faithful devotion and unrepining self-sacrifice; for the exercise of the noblest virtue, or of the gentlest kindliness; for the award of mercy, and of pardon; for the oblivion of wounding offences: in fact, for the development of that true and deep love, which does not shrink from a whole life of meek servitude.

[This address was written after the perusal of an excellent sermon on the same subject.]

II.

MODERATION.

My dear children.

In the whole circle of human failings there are scarcely any against which you have not been anxiously cautioned; there are none of which you have not been told how easily they may lead to vices whose entanglements become, indeed, heavy chains, and render the enjoyment of happiness impossible; there are none of which you have not heard how rapidly they may deepen into sin, and thus foreshadow a whole life of suffering and sorrow. On the other hand, there is surely no quality which has not been placed before you as a lamp of brilliancy to throw light upon the most rugged, the most difficult path, to help you in the fulfilment of duty, and guide you to the goal of bright contentment. Let us hope, my dear children, that no lessons have been lost; that all have sunk deeply into well-disposed minds, and induced you to shrink from evil; that they have been treasured by warm and generous hearts, and have kindled enthusiasm and admiration for every great aim, for every good deed. And yet, strange and contradictory as it may seem, it is of the utmost importance to warn you, my dear children, lest you should, even in the exercise of the best feelings, drift unconsciously into exaggeration. Singular as it probably appears, it is, nevertheless, perfectly true, that our noblest qualities, if developed to excess, may lead us astray, and plunge into difficulties and disappointments, not merely ourselves, but what is perhaps far worse, those whom we should strive to delight and to benefit.

It has most truly been said that " Moderation is the silken thread running through the pearl chain of all virtues."

Moderation connects the qualities which, instead of being scattered and lost, thus adorn a whole life. Among them, and especially in connection with the best attributes of women and young maidens, patience occupies, if not the highest, the foremost rank, as nothing can be more quietly useful than the unpretending submission which bows without a murmur to the daily and inevitable trials and troubles of life; nothing can be more softening than the gentleness which, in the home circle, overcomes all difficulties of temper and disposition, and causes cheerfulness to smile round the domestic hearth; for surely, even those who are habitually harsh and stubborn in word and action, become unwittingly vanquished by the mild sway of calm serenity. It is, indeed, like the warm sunshine of the fable that caused the chilly way-farer to relinquish his protecting cloak, which the most violent efforts of the raging wind had been unable to tear off.

Yet patience may be carried too far, and degenerate into weakness. It may disable us for the duty of withstanding injustice and tyranny; it may cause us to endure an existence of suffering, while calm yet firm opposition might secure for us a life of enjoyment; it may transform our active powers for good into the mere passive habit of endurance and into the dull capacity of bearing rebukes and affronts; it may encourage and develop the faults of others. If patience deserves praise among the pearl chaplet of virtues, persever-ance receives even a larger share of approbation, because it appears to shine in alliance with constant and well-sustained exertion; and, at first sight, it would seem almost impossible to tear the silken thread which binds it to the sister qualities—for who can hope to succeed, or who deserves to win any prize without constant industry, without indefatigable assiduity, without the eagerness that lends wings to the homely painstaking, without persistent activity, without unflagging readiness to go on—to move forward, whether the object

be to acquire knowledge, to win applause and
fame, or to serve individuals or large communities. And yet perseverance may overstep the
boundaries of utility. It ceases to merit admiration when it is blunted into drudgery; it ceases to
be praiseworthy when the animating spirit droops
and vanishes, when it becomes purely mechanical,
moving automaton-like through the day, losing
sight, in its methodical round of occupations, of
other duties, other obligations; or when it is over-
excited into restlessness, when it assumes the form
of perpetual agitation, of feverish haste, which
cannot know that repose during which the highest
thoughts are matured, and the noblest resolves
take root and are warmly cherished.

And does firmness require the guard of moderation? Is not its own immobility a rare advantage? When vacillation is swayed by every passing
breath, like the flame of a candle; when hesitation
may mar the success of a whole life; when un-
steadiness counteracts innumerable excellent purposes; when ever-changing mobility annihilates all
prospects of advancement; when inconstancy deals
blows and inflicts wounds which regret and remorse
are often unable to heal; when fickleness of taste
and disposition renders natural talents and good intentions nugatory: can firmness be a virtue which
requires moderation? Yes, my dear children, for
it is possible to carry even firmness too far. Not,

however, if by it is meant that uncompromising
tenacity of will, which adheres to every rule of
conduct, that has been well considered and carefully weighed in the balance of right and wrong;
nor that self-control which resists all temptations
and all blandishments, however enchanting they
may be; nor unswerving fidelity to friends, whatever their position; nor that self-reliance which
abides by its own conscientious opinions, heedless
of worldly consequences; nor the determination
ever to render complete justice to others, and to
remain unshaken in the fulfilment of duty. Yet
firmness may degenerate into obstinacy, and thus
check improvement; it may oppose a dead wall to
advancement, a sterile adamantine rock to the
precious seeds, which, in a better soil, would produce flowers of beauty and fruits of sweetness. In
the world of politics it has sometimes been observed
with regret and censure that statesmen have not
remained true to their creed and their principles,
and that a long life has often been unfavourably
marked by great changes of opinion. Yet it would
scarcely be possible, without obstinacy and narrow-
mindedness, to maintain a perpetual and complete
immutability of ideas. The development of civilisation, and, indeed, the progress of every passing
year must bring forth alterations in the condition
of human affairs: such changes and strides cannot
but modify the convictions of legislators, and cause

them to amend or abrogate old laws, and frame
new ones, suited to different times and altered
circumstances. Indeed, whatever our place in
the world, the waves of life will carry us gently,
or rapidly, or perhaps imperceptibly, along; the
obstinate alone, self-willed and inflexible, who are
morally blind and deaf, who see not, and hear
not, and heed not, are left behind.

And justice! can that overstep the boundaries
of moderation? Surely not, if by it we mean
perfect equity—fairness that must win all well-
balanced minds, admirable fitness in all things,
and complete impartiality. But even justice without the companion pearl linked to it by the silken
chain of moderation, justice without mercy, which
signifies pity, forbearance, sympathy, indulgence,
and oblivion, may be nought but a sharp and
relentless sword.

Let us not, however, forget that we may be too
merciful, and, by indiscriminately granting abso-
lution, render amendment impossible. And
energy, which is almost synonymous with ability,
with force and might, with the power of con-
trolling our fellow-men, and, to a certain degree,
of ruling events, of swaying and holding in subjection whatever we wish to master, whatever we
are desirous of accomplishing, does not the exercise of it require moderation? For is it not too
easily tempted to resort to harshness and to arbi-

trary means? And prudence, which seems as if
it could never be carried beyond the verge of
good feelings and useful actions; prudence, which
for our children and our friends, for those en-
trusted to our care and for ourselves, causes us to
guard against every possible danger; which makes
us discreet in word and deed; cautious lest we
should divulge secrets, evince curiosity or anxiety,
defeat pending negotiations, mar important ar-
rangements, and prove perhaps that silver is,
indeed, the inferior metal, whereas silence is gold:
can prudence require moderation? Yes; for
reserve may become excessive, and check or
destroy open-heartedness; it may act as a bar to
candour, to frankness, to sincerity, not merely
with regard to the wary and cautious themselves,
but it may have the same influence upon those
with whom they are brought into contact. Ever-
calculating prudence repels confidence, and stifles
the effusion of much harmless joy, and mirth, and
happiness.

And watchfulness in health and in sickness, at
home and abroad, in your own households, near
the cradle of the infant, while following with
loving eye the frolicsome games of childhood, or
superintending the studies and endeavours of
youth—can that stand in need of moderation?
It seems so; for the ever-vigilant, the Argus-eyed
may become suspicious, and suspicion poisons the

very life-blood, and fills every hour with torturing pangs.

Can the dictates of conscience ever be carried
too far? Is it possible to do wrong by listening
to that soft, clear, unerring voice, which never
leaves us from the time when our reason first
dawns to the last wakeful moment of our existence?
It is grievous to think that its twin virtue—zeal—
may cause it to overstep the line of duty. Vehe-
ment emotion, uncontrollable eagerness, glowing
fervour, are known to have frequently led, especially
in matters of religion—those most sacred interests
of life—to interference, and even to intolerance.
Those who feel thus impelled to question the
creed and faith of others, are apt to forget that
such points of belief and of reverence are matters
between man and his Maker, not to be searched
into by human eyes.

Even enthusiasm, which makes the heart beat and
glow for all that is great and noble, and often lifts
it above the vicissitudes of daily life into bright
spheres of hope and joyful expectation, may be so
completely dazzled as to lose itself in shifting
cloudland, and overlooking stern realities, to rush
headlong into wild, impracticable, and even dangerous schemes.

Liberality, which is free and large-hearted, and
generosity, another name for the most chivalrous
spirit, for heroism and magnanimity, for the feeling

that acknowledges and admires greatness and noble elevation of character in others, and is ever striving to give praise, time, labour, and wealth, may be perverted into extravagance, into lavish expenditure of treasure and of unmerited rewards. Charity, which represents human excellence in its highest essence, with its overflowing streams of milk of kindness, with benevolence ever hastening to do good, and never weary of works of beneficence and of self-denial, may be productive of harm, if misled by pleading compassion into indiscriminate almsgiving, which destroys independence, fosters careless habits and indolence; it may countenance artfulness, and call into existence unblushing imposition. Even devotion and piety, holiness of life, supplications and prayers, which strengthen and purify us, and surround our earthly career with a halo of the peace and serenity of heaven, may exceed their limits by completely withdrawing our thoughts and sympathies from the cares and duties of this world.

Courage, the entire absence of fear, dauntless bravery, lion-hearted valour, may be exaggerated into bold presumption and offensive audacity. And modesty, the gentlest of all virtues, compared from times immemorial to the sweet violet which nestles under sheltering leaves that screen it from the gaze of the world, may not even that be hidden too far from the appreciation of man

—may not timorous bashfulness conceal good and great qualities completely? It is well to be un-pretending and unostentatious, but does not an excess of modesty curtail its own merits and its powers of usefulness? Those who are uncon-scious of their own value—though no doubt the case is rare—or who do not prize it sufficiently, lose innumerable opportunities of developing their abilities, and of rendering true service to others. And humility, when an equivalent for unrepining submission to the will of the Most High, for tranquil obedience to inevitable and impene-trable decrees, is surely a pearl beyond price: yet humility among our fellow-beings should be held in check by moderation. For it may look like the absence of self-esteem, and wear the garb of humble resignation, while in reality it covers the sufferings of a wounded heart; it may thus be quite misunderstood, and perhaps encourage the proud, the wayward, or heedless, in their utter disregard of our feelings.

My dear children, it would indeed be delightful if we could hope to tread the paths of life adorned with the pearl-chain of all virtues; but be these brightly gleaming gems few or many, they are in peril of becoming scattered, or even irretrievably lost, without the silken and protecting string of Moderation.

III.

UNSELFISHNESS.

My dear children.

There are some faults, whether inherent in us or acquired, upon which we are apt to look, if not with complacency, as being less sinful and dangerous than those of our neighbours, or than many failings that might stain and deface our moral character, at least with indulgence, because we do not believe them to be likely to injure others, or to deprive them of even an hour's happiness or enjoyment.

Among them, there is a most insidious and deluding fault, which we do not sufficiently repel, because there is, alas! nothing new or startling in its nature, because the germ is born with our birth, and, being frequently fostered by outward circumstances, often grows with our growth. It is the fault, perhaps it ought to be called the sin, of selfishness. In its origin, its sphere of 'action appears so circumscribed, so completely confined to ourselves, our own wants and wishes, tastes and habits, occupations and pastimes, that it does not in any way appear to affect others, but, on the contrary, seems to leave them entirely unharmed and unmolested, without causing any interruption in their best and favourite pursuits, without throwing a cloud over their horizon, and without casting a shadow upon the sunlight of their happiness. For it is not like envy, which tortures those who harbour it, and those who feel themselves the objects of its bitterness; it is not relentless jealousy, with its sharp fangs dealing double wounds; not malice, with its poisoned shafts and seldom-erring missiles; nor blind and undying hatred; nor fierce revenge, more implacable still in its aim; it is not double-faced treachery; not debasing fraud; not falsehood, tale-bearing, or evil-speaking. Yet the sin of selfishness to which I allude is not the less baneful because it bears a harmless appearance; for it isolates us in feeling, mind, and action from the circle of our friends, and must lead us to sacrifice the interests of others to the gratification of our own wishes.

But you will ask, my dear children, how can we most successfully wage war against our faults, and especially remove the blot of selfishness? The best weapon, believe me, is the faithful and vivid remembrance of our duties. It is impossible to fulfil them without great efforts or great privations; and by persevering in such endeavours of self-denial, by battling against intervening obstacles and difficulties, we cannot fail to do some good; for we shall constantly have noble

aims in view, and thus develop our best qualities
and powers, while we hold our faults in subjection.
The devotion to some excellent object—the most
unwavering devotion—will be the best safeguard
against the growth of selfishness. In the whole
range of our duties, there are none more ennobling
and more blissful than those obligations of true service, of regard and affection; and do not forget, that
the sacred volume declares, " A friend loveth at all
times, and a brother is born for adversity." Yes,
a friend is unalterable and unswerving in his
sympathy; his faithful attachment, so far from
languishing, seems to increase, when called into
action by the trials and sufferings of those whom
he has learnt to cherish, be they near and dear
relatives, or merely valued and beloved fellow-pilgrims on the road of life. The Holy Bible, which
abounds in admirable lessons to guide all generations in the path of duty and righteousness, offers
a most touching example of complete self-denial
and boundless devotion in the story of Ruth,
who, when repeatedly asked, nay, implored by the
poor and aged, the childless and sorrow-stricken
Naomi, to stay in her own country and with her
own people, to dwell under the protecting roof of
her mother's house, and seek solace in the endear-
ments of a fond mother's love, instead of sharing
the poverty and hardships of the afflicted, instead
of wandering forth into a strange, unknown land,

vowed to cling to Naomi in her loneliness, and
met the most earnest supplications by the following beautiful words—" Entreat me not to leave
thee, or to return from following after thee; for
whither thou goest, I will go; and where thou
lodgest, I will lodge ; thy people shall be my
people, and thy God my God; where thou diest,
will I die, and there will I be buried." My dear
children, Ruth was certainly rewarded in the end
for her self-denying devotion, for having preferred
the fulfilment of duty to the enjoyment of a tranquil home in her own land, in the circle of her
own family; but that reward she could not have
foreseen, or even hoped for. Her example teaches
us that in the easy or difficult accomplishment of
our daily obligations, we should endeavour to
divest ourselves of all interested motives and
anticipations, and that, even while making great
sacrifices, the expectation of earthly reward should
not be permitted to rob our actions of their purity,
by perhaps strengthening them with the alloy of
selfish hopes, but thus most certainly diminishing
their real value.

It is in accordance with God's beautiful and
immutable laws, which so beneficently rule the
Universe, that we should prefer light to darkness,
day to night, sunshine to clouds, smiles to tears,
and the sight of mirthful happiness to gloomy
scenes of sorrow. It is natural we should seek our

friends on all glad and festive occasions, and that every auspicious event which increases their happiness and prosperity, should claim our sympathy, and cause us to rejoice with the joyous.

It is owing to a genial impulse of our nature, that the bright days and happy occurrences graciously vouchsafed by the goodness of the Almighty, and marking with gladness the flight of time, should find us ready and eager to participate in the satisfaction and delight of our friends; that the heavenly gift of every child born unto those we love and esteem, be thought an additional blessing, and hailed with pleasure—that the confirmation of that child, changing the fond but vague hopes of anxious parents into fair promises of excellence, be a theme of congratulation—that the marriage rite, that most binding interchange of sacred vows of unselfishness, be celebrated by affectionate relatives and friends, as a great and solemn event—indeed that all festivals and festivities should find us happy and thankful partakers. All this is but natural; for it is surely delightful to behold human happiness, and to share it by the power of sympathy; and God, whose Divine hand has made this world so enchantingly beautiful, and whose Providence showers such innumerable blessings upon us, has graciously willed and permitted that light and warmth, and the flowers of brightness and sweetness, shall far exceed the cold shadows, the

threatening clouds and fierce tempests that occasion-
ally overcast the horizon. Still, the dark shadows
exist, and their gloom often falls on the best and
kindest, and most dearly beloved of our friends :
but that darkness cannot conceal them from our
own view; it should not separate them from us,
nor build up a wall between their sorrows and
anxieties, and our affection. There are scarcely
any, let us hope that there are none, who would
remain untouched and unmoved by the sufferings
of a friend; yet there are some feeble and timorous
hearts that shrink away, because it is not in their
power to rekindle expiring joy, to revive fading or
extinct happiness, to bid hope live again, and soar
on radiant pinions into future years gleaming with
visions of felicity; and because they cannot accomplish so great and blessed a change, because they
cannot help effectually, they withdraw from all
labours of love and sympathy, and fearing lest it
should be out of their power to help at all, they do not
even attempt to assuage grief and sustain fainting
courage; or if they make a feeble trial, relinquish
the undertaking in sheer hopelessness. To excul-
pate themselves they will plead, that the sight of
human suffering overpowers their strength, and
that, unnerved by painful emotions, they lament-
ably feel their utter inability to save from impend-
ing ruin, to afford solace in the hour of bereavement
and affliction, to ward off the visitation of increas-

ing infirmities, the trial of agonising pain, or the calamity of long-continued sickness; and therefore, though believing themselves to be real and true friends, they are helpless, and keep aloof. Whatever the motives alleged, and the excuses framed, such conduct, my dear children, is not justifiable. It is true, that the Almighty alone, who strikes the blow can heal the wound; but human love and human devotion are ministering angels, all-powerful to soothe the suffering and to support the drooping; and when they appear, much gloom and sadness must vanish.

There are many bodily ailments utterly incurable by the physician's art, many frightful disorders which have for centuries past baffled the skill of the most learned and most experienced, and which continue to withstand the progress of science. Doctors do not conceal the fact; the afflicted patients are made aware of it; pitying friends know and bewail it. But would there not be cruelty in leaving the unfortunate sufferers without medical advice, not indeed to cure, since that is out of the question, but to alleviate pain, to lull anguish, to smooth the pillow?

And so it is with all sufferings, with regard to the ailments of the mind as well as with respect to bodily diseases. We may be powerless to save, but not to soothe.

Let us remember, my dear children, that the

blessings which the Lord has bountifully bestowed upon us were graciously given, not merely for our own happiness, but also in order that we might make noble and unselfish use of them, and cause them to contribute to the happiness of others, or if that, alas! should be beyond even our most strenuous efforts, that they might at least be instrumental in mitigating sorrow and sadness.

While relieving the wants of the needy, we ourselves do not feel poor; while watching by the bed of sickness, we prize health; and while weeping or praying with the dying, we learn the great lesson of life. But let us return to the poor sufferers, and while dwelling nigh unto them in thought and in affection, convince ourselves, my dear children, that it is possible for even the youngest among us, to dispel some gloom, to banish some care, to gladden, be it only at intervals, the sorrows of many aching hearts. The blind, for instance, whose eyes may be closed for ever to the glorious sights of this world, and who would indeed be joyless without the devoted love of true friends, may have the dazzling wonders of creation and the charms of life brought vividly and delightfully before their mind's eye, by the voice of affection, conveying from the pages of good and wise books, glowing pictures, or thrilling tales of interest.

Believe me, my dear children, no talent is required to prove useful to the sick and the weary;
nought is wanted but the earnest wish to do good.
And, when thinking of those whom suffering may,
for many long years, have bound captive to the
narrow prison-house of their own room, should we
not hasten to their side, we, whom the blessings
of health have left free and unfettered? Should we
not give them some of our bright life? Should we
not make them participate in our joys, that their
own existence may appear less dim and dreary,
that their melancholy thoughts may flow into
other channels, and mix with clearer streams?
The loss of fortune is hard to bear; the loss of
health is a severe affliction; but the loss of
friends is the greatest of all trials, and leaves us,
humanly speaking, entirely desolate.

When loved ones are removed by the hand of
death, the void at our side can never be filled, and
the anguish of the separation no tongue can tell;
yet the sorrowing soul bows in humble resignation
to the inscrutable decrees of Providence: but
to be deserted in the hour of need, in the time
of sore affliction, is a species of suffering from
which the lacerated mind shrinks, against which
the bleeding heart revolts.

" A friend loveth at all times."

Let us prove, my dear children, that we continue to value and cherish our friends for their

own sake, and, that our affection does not melt away, because worldly advantages have ceased to encompass them, or because they have been bereft of the higher blessings of health, because sickness or sorrow has dimmed the eye, blanched the cheek, and shattered the frame of those, whose smiles, whose words, whose looks of happiness, once contributed to our enjoyment of life.

Yet there are some organisations in which pity and compassion are largely developed; there are some whose energies are concentrated in serving their friends in adversity with helpful deeds and even with every self-sacrifice that the fondest affection can suggest, but whose powers of sympathy seem exhausted or paralysed, when, after the darkness and the storm, the brilliant bow of hope once more spans the horizon of the much-tried sufferers, and the tide of prosperity and happiness returns to the impoverished and the forlorn. When no longer wanted to aid, to cheer, or to console, they stand aside, and comparative indifference replaces the warmth of feeling which had pervaded every action of their existence. They are like the nightingale, whose beautiful but melancholy strains seem to sympathise merely with the sorrowful, and whose thrilling notes wake echoes in all sad and suffering hearts; while the lark flies and floats only into regions of warmth, and light, and sunshine, and unites with all the happy and mirthful on earth, in enchanting songs of gladness. Let us, my dear children, endeavour to combine the gifts of the plaintive nightingale and the gladsome lark. It is not impossible to do so, if we strive to foster the feelings and to cultivate the mental faculties. May the latter guide and instruct us, may we learn to hearken to their warnings, and fulfil the duties of affectionate service and devotedness with all the energies of our nature, so that, with the blessing of Almighty God, we may indeed hope to be loving friends at all times, and gentle, helpful brothers and sisters to all around us.

IV.

COVETOUSNESS.

My dear children,

The Divine rules laid down for our guidance, are either laws framed to teach and bring vividly before us the manifold duties we owe to our brethren, or they are precepts intended to enforce the obligations we owe to ourselves, and which, if scrupulously fulfilled, will assuredly make us better and wiser. Though most of us have sufficient sense and knowledge to allow the importance of conscientious zeal, we sometimes fall short of the accomplishment of duty, not indeed from any doubt or scepticism, as sentiments so wrong and so sinful are seldom, or never, harboured by us, but from a latent and half-conscious feeling, that an entirely faithful adherence to precept, to the most admirable of Divine laws, is beyond our feeble powers, beyond the possibility of human achievement. Perhaps we should be less incredulous and more hopeful, my dear children, if we thought and knew, not only, that the entire fulfilment of duty brings, and indeed is in itself, the best, truest, and purest of all rewards; but if we felt also that some

of the commandments so wondrously promulgated,
and so graciously vouchsafed to all mankind
throughout all generations, are chiefly intended to
guard us personally against much suffering and
sorrow, against the torments, which quite apart
and removed from the wants and wishes, hopes,
and aspirations of others, threaten to gnaw our
hearts secretly away.   By the outward world such
mysterious torments are perhaps not even suspected, and therefore they ought to be all the more
readily overcome.

Among the commandments, intended not so
much to regulate our conduct towards those around
us, as meant for our inmost selves, the one that
claims by far the highest importance is the last
injunction of the Decalogue—"Thou shalt not
covet thy neighbour's house, thou shalt not covet
thy neighbour's wife, nor his man-servant, nor
his maid-servant, nor his ox, nor his ass, nor
anything that is thy neighbour's."   And yet it
is that behest which we are most easily and
most frequently led to infringe.   We all bow down
to the Lord God, the beneficent Creator and Preserver of heaven and earth; we do not make
graven images, nor do we worship idols in the
literal sense of the word; we avoid taking the
name of the Almighty in vain; we remember the
Sabbath, and try to keep it holy; we love and
honour our parents; and, with regard to the other

four precepts we should, indeed, be branded as great sinners and criminals if we did not live in strict obedience to them. But we find it difficult to keep the tenth commandment, or to speak more correctly, we are easily and almost unwittingly led to break it. And this occurs, because the transgression is not supposed to injure any one, because it is most frequently a hidden sin, sedulously kept back in the remotest cells of the heart, not quickly detected, and, even when discovered, not visited with the severest reprobation of the world, nor punished by the social law of any land.

True, it must always be painful to suspect, or to be convinced, that we are exciting feelings of envy, or that such sentiments are either roused or indulged by others; therefore covetous persons are avoided as we are apt instinctively to avoid the sight, the sound, or the touch of unpleasant things, such as a sharp wind, a biting frost, a creeping worm, a slimy slug, a cold clammy toad, a stinging nettle, a buzzing insect; but to be shunned is perhaps the only punishment which the world adjudges to the envious. Yet the transgression of the tenth commandment is a grievous wrong, and though scarcely any outward retaliation awaits us for it, the inward chastisement is great and lasting. It is self-inflicted torture of the severest kind; it embitters the disposition; and if envy and covetous-

ness should not subside or be conquered, the whole
life-blood of those who give way to such insidious
enemies, becomes incurably diseased and tainted.
The miserable folly and sinfulness of envy can be
easily pointed out to you, my dear children, and
you will surely lend an attentive ear to those who
exhort you to refrain from such deplorable aberrations.

When tempted by the force of circumstances,
or rather by our own weakness, to break the tenth
commandment, let us remember the unbounded
goodness of God to us all; let us recollect the
blessings vouchsafed to each of us individually, and
then compare these treasures of His beneficence
with the gifts bestowed on others. The neighbour's house may be larger, and better, and finer
than ours. But why should that fill us with
anger and bitterness of spirit? Why should not
the humblest, lowliest dwelling that shelters us
and our loved ones from howling wind, or pelting
rain, or piercing cold, from the violence of the
snow-storm, or from the glare and the scorching
rays of the sun—why should not that dear home
be the abode of contentment and happiness?

Surely youth, and health, and strength are
great treasures:—velvet hangings, soft couches, and
downy pillows may also be considered luxuries;
but they cannot be deemed the real necessaries
of life. They will not compensate us for fading

youth, for failing health, or broken strength.
After a well-spent day, a good conscience becomes
our pillow; and God, in His beneficence, sends
peaceful and refreshing slumbers to all His children wherever they seek rest, and whatever be
the roof which protects their weariness; and on
waking at early morn, the dimpling smiles, the
looks of rosy health, of fond affection and of
bright cheerfulness, which greet us in a happy
home, are far more enjoyable than any gold or
glitter or dazzling grandeur reflected by even a
thousand mirrors. We often find, and indeed we
know, my dear children, that the palaces possessed
by the so-called privileged few are not so beautiful,
are not so splendid and attractive, as those magnificent public buildings and institutions, those
museums adorned with rare and marvellous works
of art, those galleries brilliant with the paintings
of men of immortal genius, those aerial crystal
structures so full of wonders from all climes, which
millions of human beings, and you, with many
others, may admire and enjoy. And remember
also, that the beauties of nature far outshine the
most perfect achievements of art. Those beauties,
which the bounty of the Lord has created for the
benefit and enjoyment of all His children, are
infinitely more fascinating and enchanting than
any feeble representation of them on walls or
canvass by the hand of man can possibly be.

There is no artist—there never was one—who could rival by the skill of his pencil the light-bringing loveliness of the rising sun, emerging from a bed of roses; the freshness of the morning hours, which bathe the waking world in pearly dew; or the calmer brightness of a starry night, delighting and soothing us after the labours of the day.

But perhaps you will think, my dear children, that the contemplation of all this might be yours, with the possession of youth, health, strength, mirth, and hope, and that you yet could own a dwelling similar to the envied neighbour's house, with all its comforts and luxuries. But the Almighty has wisely ordained that there should be no equality of worldly possessions on earth. If all were equally prosperous, there would be fewer motives for exertion—there would be incalculably less emulation, less ambition—there would be no improvement, and, comparatively speaking, no labour, which gives zest to our days and strength to our powers. And, as progress is the great and admirable law of the universe, the stagnation of all human energy would soon lead to indescribable confusion and misery; the reaper would not cut the corn, the husbandman would leave the heavy plough, and each person would be so completely engrossed, and so entirely occupied in satisfying his own cravings, that the decay of all the arts of civilisation would become inevitable.

"Thou shalt not covet thy neighbour's man-servant, nor his maid-servant, nor his ox, nor his ass, nor anything that is thy neighbour's."

Not only ought you to abstain, my dear children, from coveting what may be bought or sold, from coveting your neighbour's rich pasture-lands and the cattle that browse thereon, his golden wheat-sheaves at blessed harvest-time, and his purple grapes in the glowing vintage season, but you should also abstain from coveting those far greater, far more valuable treasures, which can be neither bought nor sold. In sickness, let us not envy the healthy; nor, when bodily weak or infirm, covet the strength of the robust; nor, in declining old age, envy the bright hopes of the youthful. We should remember that the most blooming flower may harbour in its calyx an insidious enemy, that the fury of the blast, or the maiming flash of lightning, may destroy the proudest oak, and that the scythe of death often mows down the youngest and fairest in the rich promise and beauty of early youth.

You may have seen, on some bright sum-mer's day, trees green and flourishing, eagerly sought by sweetly singing birds, illuminated by the rays of the sun, and forming, as it were, bril-liant emerald temples pervaded by melodious song;

one furious storm may pass over the garden and hurl the noblest branches to the ground, leaving nought but ruin behind, while the lowlier and almost stunted shrubs may grow and thrive, and expand into luxuriance.

But it is not merely futurity that is hidden from our eyes; much also of that which is going on silently around us remains beneficently concealed from our view. We may be tempted to envy talent, success, or fame, but we cannot read the hearts of the gifted, of the successful, or of those who appear to have reached the pinnacle of greatness. Their hard struggles, their bitter pangs, their oppressive anxieties and disappointments, their wounding humiliations, their disenchantments, we know little or nothing of. It has been wisely ordained by Divine Providence that sighs and moans, and groans innumerable, should be suppressed or unheard. The sight of so much agony would sadden us too deeply, would dishearten us for the task of life; and the sufferers themselves would, or might, lose much of their courage, of their spirit of independence, if all the world knew their trials, and could see their anguish.

How great is the folly of the envious, how great is their sin, whatever shape it may assume! Let us hope that it seldom means the wish to deprive our neighbour, or to see him deprived, of his possessions; and that envy is chiefly a senseless longing for advantages similar to those enjoyed by others. But, nevertheless, covetousness is always wrong—wrong, because it is forbidden by Almighty God, and forbidden because it is destructive of all human happiness.

Perhaps, when originally given, the Divine commandment was as little comprehended by the Israelites in the wilderness as, in our own days, warning words—prohibitions of a loving parent—would be understood by a young and inexperienced child. God our Father forbids us to be envious and covetous, because envy cankers the heart and makes us wretched by rendering impossible the enjoyment of that which we really possess, by misdirecting our exertions, our thoughts, our feelings. Though every blessing comes from God, it has been ordained by Him that we should owe contentment and happiness to our own efforts, to the fulfilment of duty; and that the possession of the greatest advantages should be marred and rendered nugatory by the infringement of duty and the commission of sin. Never think, never talk, my dear young friends, with envious feelings of the treasures of others. Be grateful for all that has fallen to your share. God, the universal Father, disinherits none of His children; but He has decreed that there should be throughout the world infinite varieties of gifts, of pursuits, and of position, endless degrees of abilities and of

acquirements. Some live and toil in humble hamlets, others labour in proud cities; some work
with skilful hands, others with the powers of the
mind; but all should labour most strenuously to
pluck out envy and covetousness from their hearts
—all should learn to rejoice in the happiness of
their neighbours, and feel themselves happy and
privileged in being permitted zealously and
anxiously to minister to its widest diffusion.

V.

FAMILY WORSHIP.

My dear children.

When there is no harrowing sickness, no overwhelming affliction under our roof, to keep us prisoners within the narrow boundaries of the house, to shut us out completely from the external world—when cares may be said to weigh lightly upon us—when we can cast aside with our work-day clothes the occupations, the struggles, and disappointments of the week—when all our loved ones are well and robust, and all may cluster around us, to seek the road to the temple on the holy Sabbath—then it may indeed be delightful to bow down in the hallowed edifice, where hundreds of worshippers lay their thanksgivings at the foot of the throne of Eternal Mercy; where hundreds of hearts send their most ardent prayers to our Creator and Preserver, the Fountain of all blessings; where the sacred scroll of Divine Writ is unfolded by pious hands; and where we may join in thrilling Hallelujahs to the Lord God Almighty with all the adoring voices that rise in

jubilant notes to praise His sacred name. But
there may be sickness or sorrow to prevent us
from venturing forth; passing ailments or abiding
infirmities to confine us within doors: shall they
render the worship of the Eternal impossible
—render it more difficult, less perfect, less true,
and less fervent?

Surely it is a touching and soul-stirring sight,
that of a loving family, when all the members lift
up their voices and their thoughts, their prayers,
their hopes, and their most secret aspirations, to
the Highest and Holiest, to the Almighty, when
the mother prays that He may give life and
health, unclouded innocence and prosperity to her
children—when the father invokes the blessings
of Divine Providence upon the heads of his sons
and daughters, and offers supplications to the
King of kings for the happiness of his house—
when little children lisp all the fondest words of
their pure young hearts to the invisible and bountiful Benefactor in heaven, asking Him to bless
their parents, their brothers and sisters, and all
the affectionate friends who form their world, who
are their ministering angels on earth. The early
prayer, so gently pervaded by the soft influence
of the by-gone night with its refreshing and invigorating slumbers, seems to waft peace and
tranquillity throughout the house, to inaugurate
the day with the light of cheerfulness, with the

warmth of hope, with the glow of good and earnest resolves.

But, when no imperative home duties intrude to keep us under our own roof on the Sabbath day, it is surely one of our highest obligations and of our greatest privileges to seek the temple of the Lord.

Public worship, in the presence of the Almighty, in the sacred precincts dedicated to His holy name, brings us into closer communion with all around us. It is certain to impress upon us more vividly—if any outward circumstances or all-absorbing pre-occupations or personal anxieties should have obscured or effaced the truth from our minds—that before the immeasurable greatness of the Lord, we are all equal—all equally small—yet, by His unbounded goodness, all equally and lovingly cared for; it is certain to remind us of the wider duties, which in humblest imitation of infinite beneficence and mercy, each has to fulfil according to his finite means and poor capacity. Moreover, the words and admonitions of the preacher, may bring clearly before us some faults and failings of which we were but dimly aware or felt but vaguely guilty; may awaken and rouse into activity some noble qualities, clouded perhaps by the cares of every-day life; while the voices of those who pray around us, and the sacred hymns which fill the holy edifice, raise us into a sphere of calm contemplation and

D

sacred peace, before which all the shadows of the
earth fade away. Still we are bound to confess,
how often this holy influence vanishes alas ! even
on the threshold of the shrine ; how soon and how
inevitably we must return to the daily and hourly
occupations of our life and to our household
cares ; how small a portion of our time is given to
even the longest service; how quickly the most
gentle or most impressive words of reproof and advice may be obliterated from our memory and our
breast; how soon our tears, the bitter and scalding
tears of remorse and repentance, may dry, and our
vows be forgotten, or lose their binding and
sacred power, unless we recall their import,
unless we strengthen them by daily prayer and
worship at home.

And how invigorating, yet how softening, is the
prayer in the circle of each private family; how
tranquillising are the devotions of each when the
father and mother, so to say, become the priest
and priestess of the Eternal, and the same roof,
under which we enjoy the gifts of the Almighty's
goodness, and where smiles of joy have wreathed
our lips, or sighs of sorrow escaped from them,
where our happiest hours have been passed, where
the pangs and trials of sickness have alternated
with the blessings and delights of health—the
same roof which holds perhaps our death-bed,
becomes a temple dedicated by loving hearts on
earth to the Fountain of all love in heaven.

In the dew-gemmed morning hour we lift up our hands to give humble and fervent thanks for the refreshing slumbers of the night; and, when the shadows of evening have fallen, we express our deep gratitude for the day which has passed by, and brought the boon of health, and warded off sore sickness and suffering, while from innumerable thousands of homes similar prayers and thanksgivings rise in the stillness of the night to praise the holy name of the Omnipotent. The good effect which the habit of praying has upon little children, can hardly be defined or overrated. Before they may even be able to understand its value and its power, they learn that for all gifts, and all joys, and all treasures, they owe thankfulness to the great unseen Benefactor; thus gratitude and appreciation are the first feelings they are taught, though the words which express these sentiments may be far above their comprehension. It is desirable that the solemn words of supplication and of thanksgiving, pronounced by old and young, should not become a mere mechanical exercise; and therefore the same form of prayer should not always be used. Surely very few days, if any, can be said to roll by without bringing many alterations, without working changes in our hopes and fears, wishes and endeavours, and these we may always lay, and with them our whole hearts, before our bountiful Creator and

Preserver; and, in order to place our burden at His feet, we do not require the inspired eloquence of the Bible, nor the solemn appeals of the Prayer-book; He understands us, though our speech be untutored; even though our joy or our sorrow be inarticulate, He can hear and see it all.

Better one fervent thought, or one sigh of contrition, than a long prayer without piety, than thousands of words falling from never-tiring lips when the mind does not attend, when the soul is dormant, when the tongue repeats expressions, which habit has rendered so familiar as to rob them of their true meaning. But, my dear children, though a few simple words spoken with faith and humility, love and hope, surely travel to the throne of the Almighty, never let us turn away from the excellent books, from the admirable discourses, in which the good and the wise have enshrined their worship of the Lord; on the contrary, let us read, consult, and study them eagerly, anxiously, and deeply. They will increase our devotion by their beauty and power, while the thoughts and feelings embalmed in their pages will awaken and strengthen our own, and lend words and wings to those sentiments and emotions which, if not indefinite and feeble, were perhaps hopelessly struggling for outward form and utterance.

And if this applies to us all, let no mother

forget, that it is her own especial duty to teach
her children to pray, not merely out of the leaves
of even the best of books, but also out of the clear
depths of their young and innocent hearts. Yet
let us also recollect, my dear friends, that it is
not requisite, nor even right, to be always pro-
nouncing the name of the Almighty; it is not
well that our mouth should always invoke His
holy name, though it ought to dwell for ever in
our breast. Indeed it is omnipresent : its significance and the sanctity of the Lord surround us.

What is destiny, of which we hear so much?
our existence on earth, with its vicissitudes as
decreed by the Eternal. Or what is our doom? perhaps one episode embodying the crowning event of
a life which we hold by Divine behest. What our
lot ? the portion vouchsafed to us by His will; our
share ?—the sphere of our duties and enjoyments,
as marked out for us by the merciful Father; our
burden?—the weight of cares, anxieties, and sorrows,
that detach us from this world and make us readier
for the Kingdom of Heaven. What is the entire
magnitude, glory, and beauty of nature, with its
endless powers, untold treasures, and undying
charms? it is the revelation of the Almighty. He
is everywhere. The heavens above, with the moon
and stars, the seas and mighty rivers, are but
emanations of His greatness ; the winds, the
clouds, the showers, the sunbeams, are His

messengers. We hear Him in every voice of creation. The corn that ripens for our daily bread is His gift; the water that quenches our thirst is but one drop from the ever-flowing fountain of His goodness; the whole earth is brilliantly and beautifully adorned by His will; and the loveliness thereof is pervaded by His holy Spirit. These are the indelible lessons which fond parents should make their children learn and fully understand. Yet, even the teaching from that great volume of nature, ever fresh and ever new, is not all-sufficient. The most striking lesson, the least wearisome instruction, the most touching sermon, the most persuasive advice, the least wounding reproof, will always be found, not in precepts and maxims, but in their application, in the best example, in every hour of a good life. And again let me repeat that sermons of powerful and eloquent significance in the temple of the Lord may, alas! incur the risk of being erased from the breast into which they sank, or disregarded in the busy, deafening turmoil of the world, and the good resolves and determinations to which they gave birth may be slurred over, or left to die away, unless they can be kept bright, vivid, and glowing, by the daily teaching and daily example, unless constant prayer and meditation make it impossible that we should forget our duty to the Lord, even amid the complications and cares of business, the struggles and incidents of domestic life. Each silent, but ardent and anxious prayer, must fortify us for self-improvement and purify our conscience; and the knowledge of having endeavoured to fulfil all duties, cannot do otherwise than heighten and intensify our enjoyment of life. Therefore, my dear children, let us be mindful to breathe our daily thanksgivings, and to implore the Almighty for His blessing on our thoughts, and aims, and works, wherever we may chance to be, at home and abroad, while travelling on unknown roads, or sailing over tempestuous seas, amid the silence of the desert, or in foreign lands amid the busy clamour of tongues; but let us especially remember that prayer cleanses our heart, and wafts sweet incense through our dwellings, transforming them into holy tabernacles. How could the quiet nook where we worshipped be otherwise than sacred to us? How could we be guilty of falsehood and treachery where we raised our hands in supplication to the Lord, or commit fraud and perjury where we laid our heart bare to the all-seeing and all-searching eye, or give way to hatred and malice, envy and anger, where we ventured to adore the Lord of eternal love and charity? Where could we hide ourselves, our shame, our confusion, if we had to blush before the majesty of His presence? May He be our first and constant thought, from the time when we are allowed to utter His sacred name in the arms of our mother, till the latest moment of our existence, when He becomes our last thought, and His strong, but gentle hand, leads us from this world of conflicting light and darkness into one of eternal sunshine.

VI.

CONCEIT.

My dear children,

It seems surprising, not that there is so much, but that there is any, conceit in the world; and it appears difficult to understand how intelligent minds can allow that strange growth to take root and to develop itself; for it is absolutely impossible to live, which means to see and hear, to look and listen, without discerning superiority everywhere. Even superficial observation proves to us, at every moment of the day, that those by whom we are surrounded accomplish many things which we could not even venture to attempt. Now, let us endeavour to analyse what conceit really means, and what causes us to harbour, to cherish, and to display so absurd a propensity. It must be the belief, or the illusion, that we excel in art or science, that we possess talents more rare, more brilliant, and more attractive, or information more varied, more extensive, and more profound than our neighbours, or qualities of the heart, the exercise of which places us immeasurably beyond them. But this is a ludicrous

assumption ; it proves that we are taking extravagant and unjustifiable views of the abilities
that may have been vouchsafed to us, and of their
value and importance to others. From early dawn,
when our senses shake off the trammels of sleep,
till the latest hour when the day closes with its
lessons and warnings, the hands of the clock
cannot travel far over the dial without bringing
under our notice proofs innumerable of excellence
of every kind, of services the most admirable, of
great stores of knowledge freely flung open to the
ignorant, of transcendent merit so dazzling, of
worth so true and deep, that, in comparison with
such testimony of the goodness and greatness of
others, our own capacity and our own achievements
might be supposed to appear so small indeed,
that the sense of our littleness would crush
and destroy every germ of nascent conceit. The
truth of this view might be illustrated by the
lessons we derive at the earliest hour of the day
from the perusal of the public journal which has
become one of our best, and, perhaps, most indispensable instructors, conveying information which
places under our eyes the history of the world,
and unrolling before us the heroic deeds of the most
valiant on sea and on land, the labours emanating
from the statesman's cabinet, the speech of the
patriot, the glowing eloquence of the divine, the
deliberations of legislative assemblies, the addresses

of men of science, the discoveries of the pioneers
of progress, the inventions of ingenuity and re-
search, and a comprehensive survey of everything
new, curious, and interesting devised by human
thought or wrought by human skill. Ought not
this great treasury of knowledge, I will not say to
humiliate, but to teach us how small a unit we
form in the immense sum of moral and intellectual wealth constantly enriching the globe with
the choicest and most varied gifts? Have we
ever asked ourselves if we could hope to contribute even the narrative of those achievements,
so vivid, so faithful, and yet so concise, or the com-
ments on the great questions that agitate the world?
Have not the magazines, those ephemerals, taken
up perchance to lighten the tedium of a weary hour,
yet enshrining so many sparkling gems of wit
and humour, made us aware that their contents far
surpass our accomplishments, and could, perhaps,
not have been achieved by our most strenuous
exertions? And the poetry that charms our fancy,
and the drama, which keeps us spell-bound, and
the romance that bids us smile and weep, and
hope and fear, and love and suffer in unresisting
obedience to some magic pen, and the eloquence
from living lips that entrances us, and the music,
whose enchanting strains express what no words
can tell, and the painter's art that enshrines in
immortal beauty the deed of glory, the brow of

sublime thought, the witchery of fleeting loveliness, have they never appeared unattainable to
us, or have we in moments of bewildering conceit
believed ourselves capable of emulating such
creations ? Probably, neither song, nor play, nor
poem, nor picture, could have emanated from our
brain or from our hands. But even among those
whom Providence has graced with a dazzling
superiority, conceit would betoken a glaring
error of judgment. For are there not infinite
varieties of talent? Do not some pre-eminently-
gifted beings excel in one branch of art or science,
while others shine in a different field more adapted
to the exercise of their genius? Who shall say
whether the sculptor is preferable to the architect,
or the great painter to the inspired musician,
or the illustrious writer to them all ? or who
shall decide whether, in the realms of literature,
the historian, dramatist, poet, moralist, or philo-
sopher, carries off the brightest palm of excellence?
and are there not, and must there not always be,
endless subdivisions of beauty and of merit? No
historian could attempt to narrate every event
that has occurred from the birth of our first
parents until the present time ; no dramatist could
venture to call into glowing life every prominent
actor that has crossed the stage of the world from
the earliest era until this day ; no artist could be
equally felicitous and faithful in representing

earth and sea, nature wild and grand, foaming among torrents and mountain crags, and nature subdued by man in hamlets and cities, or the human face divine, the most alluring and captivating of all. But, my dear children, not only pages, but volumes, might be written, and yet they would leave unexhausted the theme of the innumerable gradations, peculiarities, and aptitudes, required to attain eminence and unqualified superiority in all the numberless varieties of works of talent and of genius. And if this applies to the really distinguished, to the great, who win wreaths of unfading laurel, why should you, my dear young friends, unknown and untried, on the threshhold of life, be conceited? Because you have perhaps learnt to read more fluently, to write more quickly, to understand more readily, to commit to memory more faithfully, to answer less bashfully than those around you? But you forget that these advantages may be the result of earlier and more regular training, of better examples at home, of stronger health, or of somewhat greater natural facility. You should not underrate such advantages; they are precious and not trifling, for they may, if carefully developed, prove of immense benefit to your friends and to yourselves; but they are, at best, mere faint and glimmering promises of future merit; how should they, therefore, give rise to conceit? Still less ought moral attributes, valuable qualities of the heart, actively transformed into untiring zeal and devotion, and true, unwearied charity, cause presumption to spring up, as you must remember, my dear children, that, although talent may not be possessed by many, the pearl chaplet of virtues belongs to all who will dive for the precious gems into the recesses of the soul, and wear and keep them bright and spotless.

We may be humble-minded and entirely free from senseless vanity and foolish conceit, and yet not ungrateful for any peculiar capacities or qualities that may have fallen to our share; indeed we cannot be too thankful for them, or prize them sufficiently. But judicious appreciation is not conceit; it never rises to the surface, either offensively or ludicrously; it pervades our inmost being with the anxious desire to make the noblest use of all advantages, be they moral, intellectual, or even corporeal, such as health and strength, and the physical power of endurance.

It has been said, with great truth, that conceit is to nature what paint is to beauty; it is not only needless, but impairs what it would improve. Painting, when unsuccessful, is certainly absurd and disfiguring; and even where it succeeds most, though perhaps showy and effective, lacks that harmony which bids features, colouring, and expression combine to mark the freshness of spring, the glow of summer, the steady light of

autumn, the paling tints of winter; it lacks that
harmony which does not conceal the traces of
care and sorrow, the indication of thought and
feeling.   Paint is always more or less ludicrous, a
sure sign of weakness; far from displaying a quality,
it obviously hides a defect or blemish.   And the
same may with truth be said of conceit.   Vanity
casts a false light over our real gifts, and tends to
dwarf those talents which, if left in their natural
simplicity, would receive their due meed of approbation.   Conceit is a mask, which renders it
difficult to know what lies underneath, and makes
it impossible to form a just estimate of the wearer.
It is not a cloak that covers sins, but a thick veil that
shrouds the original and imperishable charms of
nature.   To be conceited is perpetually to challenge
the admiration of others; it is to have no model
but ourselves, and, in that case, we seldom improve.   Possibly we may, though with much reluctance, fathom our faults, and learn thoroughly
to understand them; but we do not and cannot
form an entirely accurate conception of our aptitudes.   And, indeed, it is only by watching the
perfections of others that, having discerned in
what measure we are faulty, we may hope to
remedy our short-comings, and to increase our
attainments.   Conceit not only checks progress,
but completely stops it.   The conceited cannot
strive after excellence; if not so brilliantly

successful as their own inordinate vanity would lead
them to expect, they accuse the world of injustice
or blindness, perhaps of envy or prejudice, for
conceit is very different from love of approbation ;
the latter delights in winning golden opinions,
while the former believes itself superior to its
judges.   A painted lady returns to her mirror,
astonished and annoyed to find that cosmetics
and artifice have not imposed upon society a laborious counterfeit for a fascinating reality ; and, in
the same way, the conceited are astounded that
they do not meet with the praise and the admiration which they covet.   But, my dear children,
truth, if not always attractive, is always preferable
to falsehood.   Paint and conceit are perplexing
masks.   Truth may be painful at times, but
the pain suggests remedies or palliatives, whereas
a sham deceives the vain man himself, and leaves
him helpless.   Those who live and move behind
such fictions, have placed, as it were, a wall between
themselves and the great world of truth—a wall
that screens them from the all-revealing lights,
which, doubtless, divulge many faults, yet divulge
them only in order strongly to demand their
removal—lights whose clear rays are so eagerly, so
anxiously, and so perseveringly sought and valued,
because no day elapses without proving what
priceless treasures they add to the sum of human
happiness.

VII

OUR MOST PRECIOUS POSSESSIONS.

MY DEAR CHILDREN.

It seems almost invidious to warn you against dangerous habits, of which we may hope there are few examples among us, such as the bad taste of taking undue pride in bodily or mental advantages, in wealth, in territorial or any other possessions. It is, perhaps, not merely the impression of good lessons and wise counsels, which even the most self-satisfied remember, and even the so-called favourites of fortune recollect and obey, when they refrain from vaunting their real or imaginary superiority ; they bow, although it may be unconsciously, to the dictates of time, of progress, and of civilization, when careful not to betray, either by word, look, or manner, an assumption of greatness or pre-eminence.

They do not audibly exult in their prosperity lest they should wound the sensitiveness of others ; they make no vain-glorious display for fear of exciting ill-will or bitterness of spirit, and they are right not to obtrude themselves and their position on the notice of the surrounding circle, for such self-parading is a very hateful

species of egotism.   Scrupulous regard for the
feeliugs, for the circumstances, and even prejudices of those among whom the existence of the
well-favoured is spent, seems good and desirable
in itself, but it is perhaps scarcely sufficient to
preserve or shield us against the belief that the
possession of splendid treasures forms an impregnable tower of strength, and to remind the prosperous that the earth, with all the fulness thereof,
is the Lord's, whilst human beings are only frail
and transitory tenants, liable to removal at any
time.   For does not parching drought, or cease-
less rain, the raging storm, the devastating fire,
or the overwhelming flood, destroy glowing vineyards and teeming corn fields, uproot the noblest
trees, sweep houses and whole cities away ? Do not
wars and revolutions, or even mere vicissitudes,
engulph princely wealth ? Is not the most brilliant
talent often obscured by sudden sickness, the
proudest eminence, the greatest power, annihilated
by an utterly unlooked for stroke, by an inexplicable change in the wheel of fortune that appears
unmercifully to crush those whom it had exalted?
Only as the faithful stewards of the Almighty's
gifts and blessings can the children of God consider themselves rich ; and if they strenuously
endeavour to make the best use of their energies
and opportunities, they will never be guilty of
open or covert boastfulness, but will cherish a

true knowledge, a heartfelt appreciation of their
duties, and make a zealous and constantly anxious
effort to fulfil them. "In all labour there is profit," says King Solomon ; the active, unflinching
exercise of our powers brings peace of mind, the
greatest of all treasures, and the axiom of the
wise monarch is probably intended to point out
the real, though frequently invisible equality
which pervades the destinies of men ; for it is the
variety of intellectual, moral, and bodily attributes
that tends to equalise the often painfully startling
differences which, at first sight, might be deemed
the offspring of grievous injustice, instead of being
the inscrutable but merciful decrees of infinite
wisdom.

It is consoling to notice the man who made himself rich, though he was destitute, and had neither
worldly goods, nor intellectual acquirements, nor
even the robust health and the iron sinews which
seem to defy the inclemency of adverse weather
and the vicissitudes of unfavourable climes. He
made himself rich, because he had been taught to
transform apathy into activity, to change sloth
into industry, despondency into perseverance,
irritability into gentle patience, and a gloomy turn
of mind, apt to dwell upon the shadows and to ignore
the lights of our terrestrial existence, into habitual
cheerfulness and smiling content. By means of
qualities so useful he is able to satisfy his own

wants and wishes, and to minister, by quiet precept and firm example, and with soothing words
and helpful deeds, to the necessities of others, so
as to cause the poor to be unrepining, the sick
hopeful, and even the dying resigned. It is less
pleasant, but perhaps equally profitable, to contemplate those who make themselves poor, though
cradled in luxury. They should bear in mind
the sons of the old husbandman, who, on his
death bed, had promised to leave a priceless
treasure. The survivors expected a miser's hoard,
countless bags of money and coffers of gold, and
deemed themselves utterly poor because the chests
and granaries of their father were completely
empty. In the lowliest of houses, where pomp
and luxury had always been unknown, they
looked in vain for gold and jewels. Disappointed and discouraged, they yet felt un-
willing to doubt the truthfulness of dying lips.
The dwelling was ransacked from the garret to
the cellar, yet without any success. In searching
the roofs, the walls, and the floors of the crazy tene-
ment, the house itself was demolished, no portion
of it appeared worthy of being retained; but
before the disappointed heirs left the unpromising
property, they determined upon examining most
diligently every inch of the surrounding fields,
which seemed quite barren, and had indeed long
been allowed to lie fallow. It cost much time

and labour and indefatigable perseverance to explore every rood of ground; no stone was left
unturned; all the tools and implements employed
by farmers and gardeners were used in search of
the hidden treasure. Spade and pick-axe did
their work; springs, long-neglected, were re-
discovered; always in quest of concealed gold,
the plough and the harrow passed over the land;
heaps of pebbles were removed, rank grasses annihilated, the root of every tree was sedulously
examined: thus all became cleansed, purified, and
fertilised by incessant care, labour, and attention.
As years glided on—so says the time-honoured
allegory — and the once barren ground was
changed into orchards, laden with rich clusters
of fruit, into gardens fragrant with blooming
flowers, into fields waving with golden harvests;
and when the long-neglected acres had become
pasture lands covered with snowy flocks and
goodly herds: then the sons understood the significance of their father's last words, and felt that
he had indeed left them a precious inheritance.

My dear children, our heavenly Creator has
more than promised, He has bestowed upon us
great riches, but we must labour to deserve them;
and, like the heirs of the old farmer, we must
work indefatigably to employ them well. The
human heart may indeed become or remain a
barren and stony field, overgrown with rank

weeds; but care for its best germs, and attention to the development of its full powers, will soon make it a beauteous garden, bright with living fountains, and indescribably rich with priceless possessions, with those trees of wisdom which yield the best fruit—with the firmness that withstands the most bewildering temptations, with the courage that confronts the most appalling dangers, with the energy that overcomes the most towering obstacles, with the fortitude that calmly bears all trials and sorrows, with the gentle pity which commiserates the suffering, with the mercy that forgives, with the charity that has balsam for all wounds, and with the love that covereth all offences. Firmness—as distinguished from obstinacy—is the offspring of deep convictions, determined to resist brilliant allurements, which are mere baits and snares; firmness opposes its invincible rocks to the blandishments held out by soft repose; when activity is demanded from us, or when duty calls for indefatigable exertions, it places its iron defences between our weakness and the most delightful attractions of pleasure. It warns and exhorts us to stand upright and to persevere when disappointments dash our brightest hopes to the ground, and would lay us prostrate by the side of our shattered expectations. Courage enables us to cope with all perils, to be fearless in every good cause, to go forth and wage war against all enemies —not exactly against foes in human shape or personal display of ill-will and ill-feeling — the days of single combat are past—but against innumerable enemies in the form of vice and sin, of dark, obdurate ignorance, of contemptuous pride, and disdainful prejudice. And if courage enables us to defy danger, and to rush boldly and fearlessly into the midst of it, energy, undaunted by defeat, wrestles powerfully with living obstacles, and is triumphant in the end; while fortitude bears with tranquil resignation an almost crushing load of care; and pity, mercy, charity, and love walk hand in hand to scatter happiness around, and to be delightfully rewarded by joyful smiles of gratitude.

Do not, my dear children, suppose that it can be thought useful for you to undervalue or despise the possessions that are by general consent deemed real treasures, such as wealth, which, generously and judiciously employed, blesses him that gives and him that receives; or, better still, great and dazzling talents, the exercise of which ennobles the possessor, and enriches the world with beautiful and beneficent works of genius, art, and science; yet such possessions form exceptions to the rule, and the generality have to dig and delve like the sons of the husbandman. But that should not cause us to murmur or to repine ; for labour is the salt of life, and activity itself is one of the conditions that lead to its enjoyment. No man can tell how great are the powers enshrined in his heart and soul until he has endeavoured to develop them to the utmost of his ability. There may be mines deep and rich which, liberated from overlying impediments, will yield up their gold ; there may be hidden sources which, released from surrounding obstacles, may gush forth, lavishing abundant benefits, and spreading them far, far beyond the immediate circle of their possessors.

And once more be reminded, my dear children, that not the most costly gems and jewels of earth and sea, not the fairest flowers, not the sweetest fruits, not the most splendid talents, not the rarest gifts of the Almighty's bounty, are the best and greatest favours which His paternal hand bestows on mortal man, but that, on the contrary, the most general of His blessings are by far the most precious—that bread and water to nourish and refresh us—that our senses, through which we see the outer world, and learn to admire its beauties and appreciate its wonders—that the swiftness and aptitude of our limbs—health, the great centre of all enjoyment—and the heart, thrilling with every tender feeling or noble sentiment—are the best treasures which His boundless beneficence bestows upon His children.

Let us then in all humility cherish them with thankfulness, and with a due sense of their infinite value; let us use them constantly, yet carefully, and show and teach to those around us how un-rivalled is their worth, and how inestimable are the benefits they secure to all mankind.

VIII.

DEVOTED SERVICE.

My dear children.

Whether we live in proud cities, encompassed by works of art and science, or dwell in quiet hamlets amongst woods and fields, or near the ever-flowing and ebbing waves of the ocean, we cannot listen to the voices around us, nor let our eyes rest on the products of civilisation, and on the far greater gifts so lavishly bestowed by bountiful nature, without feeling that nothing exists which has not been most graciously designed by Divine Providence to do good and varied service. Indeed one day will suffice us to feel that the mere grains of sand on the beach are probably not more numerous than the tenants, than the productions of the seas with their well-known uses and their yet unknown utility and application; from the gigantic whale to the phosphorescent animalcule that dots the waters with its brilliancy ; from the coral islands and beds of pearl and treasures of amber to the translucent pebbles which little children gather on the shore ; from the far-extending submarine forests, and the leaves and flowers of the sea, with their

health-restoring cordials and glowing dyes, and
strengthening salts and indestructible metals, to
the smallest drop of water in the fringe of the
ocean. All of these—field, woodland, and garden,
blossom and fruit, seed-pod and grass-blade, twig
and bark, even the insect that shapes the oak-leaf
into its cradle—yes, one and all, have been called
into existence, and formed by infinite and beneficent wisdom, to yield service to the great family
of man. And if we have abundant, nay, irrefutable reason to believe that nothing is useless,
although whole generations of travellers and philo-
sophers may yet spend centuries, nay thousands
of years in discovering the hidden meaning of
every object in heaven above, or on earth beneath,
it is impossible for one single moment to delude
ourselves into the belief that we alone, the highest
of organised beings, for whose benefit and delight
all these gifts and powers were granted and
framed, for whom this boundless service of nature
was formed, that we should not also be called
upon, and in a far wider sense and loftier sphere,
to enter the great public service of mankind. Do
not misunderstand me, do not think that your
attention will be called to mere activity and industry; you well know, my dear children, how
dull and wearisome the day would be without
occupation, without business, without diligence in
accomplishing some work self-imposed, or confided

by others to our hands. But it is grievous to
see how alarming a sound the word service has
for many minds and hearts, and how brightly
independence seems to beckon to most persons
among us. Many misconceptions and blinding
prejudices exist on both subjects; and the friends
who endeavour to dispel these prejudices, and to
make the illusions connected with them vanish,
will prove their real appreciation of our needs.
To be actively, conscientiously useful to our
fellow-men, to render true and due service to
society or to individuals, should be our constant
endeavour, our pleasure, our satisfaction, and our
happiness ; the more efficient these services are,
or the more widely diffused, the more successful
is our life. By looking calmly and dispassionately around, my dear children, you will find that
all are prompted, by every voice, human and
divine, to serve others and to labour for their
advantage.   Nor are deeds of benevolence and
of charity—though they assuredly constitute the
highest forms of service—alluded to at present.
What is meant is the entire business of life,
which, in reality, when well and efficiently trans-
acted, is service of some sort.

Observe and scan the occupations and profes-
sions of those you see, or of whom you know and
read, whether they stand above or below you,
or at your side, and you will find that they

are employed in serving their fellow-creatures according to their intellectual abilities and acquirements or to their bodily strength. In the army and navy, the humblest subaltern, and the most illustrious leader; the sailor that climbs to the top of the mast, and the admiral that gives the word of command; the soldier that advances to meet the enemy's ball or bayonet, and the general that, amidst the roar of cannon, plans great battles and victories—all serve alike their country and their sovereign. The surgeon and the physician, whether at the bed side of the wealthy, or in the crowded wards of the hospital, the priest, whether in the pulpit, in the homes of poverty, or the haunts of vice, teaching, helping, soothing, and healing, are alike servants of the rich and of the poor. Barristers interpreting the laws which rule society, legislators, hereditary, or elected by popular acclamation, modifying old statutes or framing new ones, serve both ignorant masses and enlightened communities. Professors, men learned in all branches of human lore, and spreading their knowledge far and wide, serve the young and the old, and extend their teaching even to unborn generations. Architects and sculptors, artists and musicians, whatever may be the degree of excellence which they have attained, serve us by the exercise of their talents or the works of their genius; and authors, whatever the field from which they cull their flowers, serve us by enlightening

and embellishing our existence with instructive
realities and beauteous fictions. Every business,
every profession, every trade, is a species of service. The fisherman that spreads his nets, the
shepherd that tends his flocks, the farmer that
ploughs his land, or reaps the golden grain of the
furrow, all who labour in the vineyard or orchard,
in mine or quarry, in town or country, in quiet
nook or bustling thoroughfare, in the solitude of
the midnight hour or in the broad glare of day,
unknown and unrewarded in the shade, or crowned
with glory in the dazzling blaze of popularity, all
who plod on in the lowliest, humblest walks of
life, or shine on the giddy eminence of thrones,
all are servants, all serve their fellow-men, not
all in the same way, not by the same means, nor
in the same degree, but all in accordance with
their peculiar fitness.

What is it then that causes so frequently the
dread of servitude, the sort of repugnance, which
makes so many of our youths and maidens turn
away from a mode of life, stigmatised by them as
humiliating and degrading? They have an unconquerable longing for that happy condition which
they call independence. But what they mean by it is
scarcely a reality. In whatever position we find ourselves we may be said to be independent, namely,
free to leave, free to relinquish an engagement, to
loosen a tie, to cast off a chain, if either should
prove too onerous, too heavy, or too galling—

provided we have always aimed at the zealous and conscientious fulfilment of our duty. We are not slaves, not bondsmen; there is no law to compel us to serve, I will not say a cruel or tyrannical, but even an unjust or capricious master. We give our time, our care, our attention, our labour; we may give still more precious possessions than these—our attachment and devotion, while we remember the words of the Bible, "A son honours his father, and a servant his master" (Malachi i. 6), for the parallel shows most clearly that there can be no humiliation in the duties of service. But independent of rules, laws, customs, obligations, and outward circumstances we can never be. The vendors who offer their goods for sale are not more independent than the domestic servants at their household labours; if they wish to be successful and prosperous, their activity must be unremitting, in order that more industrious competitors may not deprive them of the possibility of gaining a livelihood, and theirs must be a constant struggle, perhaps against the inclement season of the year, or the alarming aspect of the market. The merchant, the manufacturer, the shipowner, and even the great landed proprietor can never be independent. They bow, as we all do, to the laws of humanity, but are swayed also in their transactions by the changes in the atmosphere which influence the productive powers of nature, by the condition of buyers and sellers, and more peremptorily still, by social and political vicissitudes, by the calamities of war and the blessings of peace.

Still you may perhaps think, my dear children, that in some respects they are more independent than the domestic servant ; that they have no orders to obey; no will, no wish beyond their own to consider ; that the day is theirs, and may be employed in perfect accordance with their own inclination, or even with their whim and caprice, unshackled either by arbitrary rules or by fitful interference. Such independence is a fiction. We are all hedged in by innumerable rules and laws, and do not stand alone in the world, masters of our destiny. Careful, conscientious, unprejudiced observation, even if not extending over wide fields and distant countries, but confined to our own immediate neighbourhood, will show us that each labours for the benefit of all, and that purely selfish work or even occupation is indeed, as it ought to be, an impossibility; for, while trying to do good to ourselves, if we really succeed, we do good to others, and serve them in the best sense of the word. Even while studying our own pleasures—provided these be legitimate and not likely to injure us in any way—it is scarcely to be imagined that we do not at the same time

minister to the enjoyment of others. Truly the
whole aim of life is, or ought to be, one of usefulness, which is merely another word for service ;
and they who miss this aim, or, rather, who fail
to understand their duty, or neglect to fulfil it,
sink down to a level of insignificance, which is
indeed humiliating when we recollect that every
creature that has been brought within reach of
our powers of cultivation, yields good and valuable
service. Surely we live for a purpose ; and to
rise in the morning from a couch of unmerited
slumber, to partake of the fruits of the earth
without having earned their refreshing sweetness
cannot afford us deep or lasting happiness ; yes,
to sleep, to satisfy hunger and to quench thirst,
may be necessary functions of our terrestrial
existence, but these are not the whole aim of it ;
and they should be exercised as a preparation for
our labours, or enjoyed as a reward of our faithful
services. The whole marvellous distribution of
the globe, and of the manifold powers of the
universe, is one of usefulness. Nothing is useless.
Earth, air, fire, and water, are our servants ; they
increase our means of subsistence, our comforts,
our wealth, our enjoyments ; and we, human
beings, endowed with the light of reason and
with innumerable faculties, why should we shrink
from the thought of serving each other, why should
we deem such service a sort of humiliating, almost

degrading, inferiority? Is that which, perhaps in a mood of despondency or in a spirit of irritation and revolt, we call a yoke, more difficult to bear from one individual than from many? Is one master more exacting than a multitude? One tongue more bitter or more stinging than the thousand tongues of public opinion? What is it that you complain of in household service, my dear children? Is it at one time the monotony, at others the perplexing irregularity of it? But such is life; it is not mere machinery in which every turn of the wheel, or every movement of the shuttle, steadily helps to make some length of yarn or of web; nor is it only a journey of pleasure, through golden meads and flowery vales, over green hills, along gently flowing rivers, where every look we cast around or every step we take discloses new beauties and new charms. I am quite sure, my dear children, that there are few among us who would not gladly and readily obey the inward voice of pity and of sympathy, pleading softly and tenderly for the poor, the suffering, and the afflicted; but our feelings of benevolence and charity are not appealed to at all hours of the day, and you have already been told that it is often far easier to perform on great occasions acts of self-denial, devotion, and sacrifice, than to pass a whole life in the zealous fulfilment of ever-recurring duties. If you will, however, keep in

mind the oft-repeated truth, that there can be
no good and great and noble career that is not at
the same time one of usefulness, not merely to the
person who achieves it, but also one of true service
yielded to others, the objectionable word will lose
its grating sound, and you will have true satisfaction in filling well, in filling entirely, and in
accordance with the abilities vouchsafed to you,
the place that has fallen to your share. The more
numerous the individuals or groups of human
beings whom we are able to benefit, and to draw
into the circle of our usefulness, the greater, the
better, and the more lasting is the service we
render.

It might be said, my dear children, that,
till now, we have taken a mere worldly view of
our subject, were not worldliness and godliness
most indissolubly connected during our pilgrimage
on earth. We cannot indeed serve our brethren
without serving the Almighty, and to Him, our
Heavenly Creator and merciful Preserver, we owe
not only gratitude, worship, adoration, but the
most energetic labours of our hands, the most
ardent aspiration of heart and soul. Yet, how
can we attempt to prove our boundless reverence,
our endless gratitude? feebly and inadequately
enough — whatever efforts we may make — yet
more by deeds than by mere words of hope and
prayer and thanksgiving, by faithful service at

home and abroad, by constant service, whatever may be our calling, by active service amid the network of our duties. The most brilliantly endowed may perhaps aspire to the happiness of doing the greatest amount of good, yet all human beings, the most lowly as well as those in high places, may hope to be useful, and by thus serving their brethren on earth, serve in grateful humility their inexpressibly good Master in heaven!

IX.

ANGER.

My dear Children.

Our hopes and fears, our joys and sufferings, our trials and triumphs, our defects and our good qualities, are, indeed, closely linked to each other, and often strangely connected. It is not, therefore, in order to produce a startling contrast or a striking picture, that when endeavouring to give a lesson or to inculcate a warning, we are induced to place in a strong light before you the thorns of failure and the palms of success, the darkness of sin and the serenity of holiness, the dangers of vice and the happiness and consolations of virtue; and to dwell upon the minor shades which divide or blend our feelings, our actions, our most valuable qualities, and our most perilous faults. You have often been told that the latter are the chief cause of our misfortunes and sufferings. Let us repeat this truth to-day, and repeat also that the plea of a natural predisposition in extenuation of some glaring offence, is an excuse, which fortunately for you cannot be admitted. If great qualities are apt to become dwarfed and even to shrink away completely by not being exercised, if

inborn talents remain perfectly useless when
not sedulously cultivated, nay, even worse than'
useless, since the neglect gives rise to perpetual
regret and constant self-upbraiding, why should
not moral blemishes, why should not faults
become obliterated when carefully kept in
check, when circumscribed, when vigilantly imprisoned in the remotest, least accessible nooks of
our inward being? None of you, my dear children,
can really believe for a moment that there exists
a fatality which impels us to do wrong, or to
harbour sinful feelings. But liberty and independence, those two precious treasures, for which
you are always longing, are great and bright
realities. They exist quite as much with respect
to our faults as with regard to our qualities.
Sloth, apathy, indolence, may allow the former to
invade the best places, and to usurp the domains
sacred to pure and noble sentiments ; but what
tyranny is there that can prevent us from endeavouring to extirpate evil inclinations, to destroy
all blemishes, and to annihilate defects? You
have heard, my dear children, that weeds grow
apace, and you also know how constantly the
rapid growth of our faults has been compared
to the quick expansion of rank and noxious vegetation. The simile is old, yet none the worse for
that; it remains true in all its bearings. The
weed which often springs up over night to dis-

figure the fairest garden, may be uprooted without difficulty, and so may our faults, provided we apply to the urgent, and perhaps daily work a firm will and a vigorous hand. Among the offensive traits of an almost spontaneous development, anger is the most prominent. Do not look upon it as a venial, pardonable infirmity of temper; it is the wide-spreading cause of much suffering, and may be transformed into our daily, nay, hourly scourge. It has, therefore, been very justly observed by an illustrious poet and thinker, that, "To be angry is to revenge the faults of others upon ourselves." The word revenge has a harsh and painful sound; it seems almost impossible that we human and most erring beings should harbour the desire to punish the sinful. Even when the offence is amenable to the law, there are, I think, few among us, who would not instinctively shrink from the office of gaoler or executioner. And let us remember, that when the law vindicates the rights of the offended, there is no direct desire to cause the poor, miserable sinners to suffer; that there can exist but a threefold aim — reformation of the guilty, prevention of a similar offence, and protection of individuals and of society. But to be angry, and thus to revenge upon ourselves perhaps the insufferable conceit, the inexplicable caprice, the wounding pride, the persecuting suspicion, the

galling injustice, the narrow-minded intolerance
of others, is a perfect folly. By being angry we run
the risk of changing the offender into the offended:
for although anger exaggerates extravagantly the
fault committed or intended, yet the latter becomes
dwarfed in comparison with our senseless wrath.
For anger has justly been likened to the raging
storm which flings to the ground the brightest
blossoms of promise, destroys the vineyard and
the orchard, shatters the finest trees, and strikes
in its blind fury house and steeple, man and
beast.   It has been truly compared to the
overwhelming flood that engulphs the richest
harvests, and sweeps away whole villages with the
helpless and the infirm, the children and the aged;
or to the devouring fire that leaves nothing behind
except ashes and blackened ruins.

These comparisons seem to apply more properly
and justly to bursts of passionate resentment and
violence; but that anger which any occasion or
the slightest provocation calls forth—the anger
which burns and smoulders—resembles far more
the wasting fever and sickness, during which
the healthy action of every organ is vitiated, and
the fountain of joy transformed into a source
of suffering, during which the life-stream becomes
tainted and poisoned, and the clearness of the
mind overcast: in such a state of morbid agitation, the throbbing of the heart is pain, the move-

ment of the lips is anguish, controlled or unsup-
pressed anger pervades every thought, every
feeling, the good qualities have no room, no play,
they are dead or in a trance. Anger may not
destroy charity, generosity, devotion, kindness,
friendship, love; but surely the devotion of an
angered heart loses its gentleness, the charity and
generosity of hands quivering with anger cannot
be softly helpful; words of friendship are unable
to soothe and to comfort when they flow from an
angered tongue. Evil sentiments and good feelings
cannot actively co-exist—they neutralise each
other; therefore let us strive to overcome those
propensities which may grieve or injure our fellow-
beings, and which mar, if they do not completely
annihilate, our own happiness. Above all let us
conquer anger, if not the worst, certainly the
most foolish form of revenge, since it absurdly
inflicts punishment on ourselves for the faults
of others, overlooking the double duty, which
enjoins us generously to forgive and wisely to
forget, in order that the remembrance of sufferings and wrongs may not rankle in us, and rob
our days of peace and cheerfulness. Yet anger is
not only a folly, but often an iniquity; for in its
senseless rage it may strike friend and foe; and
who knows whether time can ever efface the havoc
caused in one moment of blind forgetfulness?

X.

"HONOUR THY FATHER AND THY MOTHER."

My dear children.

You have frequently been told that all Divine commandments graciously vouchsafed for our guidance appear closely linked together, and that the dutiful and anxious desire to obey their dictates, as they rise before our view, or sink into our hearts, gently and surely leads us to their fulfilment, causing them to remain engraven on our minds as indelibly as those inspired words written by Moses on tablets of stone thousands of years ago; words of great and precious truth, which have indeed travelled unaltered and unimpaired through all lands and through all centuries. And as the closest connection most undoubtedly exists between all the eternal commandments, it is especially evident in the Decalogue, that wonderful code of thought and wisdom, since it is obvious that the four first ordinances embody the duties towards the Lord, and the five last comprehend those towards our neighbour, while the fifth, the injunction of filial love, forms the uniting bond between the obligations humbly due to the Almighty, and those we owe to man. The deep wisdom we adore, and which is so abundantly revealed throughout the world, would seem also to manifest itself in this grouping of the primary laws. For parents are indeed the Providence of children on earth, the visible representatives of our unseen Father and Protector in heaven, and warm and devoted affection for them is the commencement, and comprises the rudiments of all our duties towards our fellow-beings.

Family life at home represents the teeming life of the great family of mankind out of doors, in town and country, in our own native climes, and far, far away in all quarters of the globe, under all circumstances of civilisation and development; for human nature is the same everywhere, and our parents form the centre of that dear home, which we have been taught and have fondly learnt to cherish. The disobedient son—unmindful of the wishes of his earliest and kindest benefactor, heedless of the voice of paternal experience, which comes to him in its gentlest, most persuasive and affectionate tones, and not, as experience is apt to meet his ear at a later period in life, with perhaps grating harshness—that callous undutiful son is not likely to become a good and devoted husband, a true and safe friend, a patriotic, unselfish member of the commonwealth, an indulgent, forbearing, and forgiving parent, a man to be trusted and relied upon for the conscientious fulfilment of more arduous duties, for the accomplishment of obligations that may perhaps severely try and tax the powers of body and soul.

The second portion of the commandment says: "That thou mayest live long in the land." The sacred text signifies, no doubt, that thou mayest continue to live well, honourably, usefully, and beneficently; that thou mayest earn the boon of life, and make noble use of it. Under the paternal roof, which is indeed a sanctuary, we serve an apprenticeship of duty, and the exercise of filial love and obedience teaches us every lesson of the heart, prepares us for the discharge of the highest obligations, of the most difficult tasks. Affection towards parents is indeed commanded to us by Divine Providence; yet it is not only enjoined by the will of Almighty God, it is also one of the earliest and most natural dictates of gratitude, begotten by innumerable words and labours of love, the ineffable power, the comforting tenderness of which we feel at every hour of the day, long before we are able to understand and to appreciate the value of them, long before we can unravel the meaning of the heavenly law.

The infant receives nourishment from the mother's breast, warmth and shelter in the mother's arms; softly cradled in them as the bird

in its nest, it is rocked there, not like the fledgling
by the swaying breeze, but by every pulsation of
the mother's heart; its feeble wailings are hushed,
its cries of weariness quieted by the gentlest
lullaby. On the mother's knees the child goes to
sleep, and feels safe there. On opening its won-
dering eyes, her smile cheers it, her words are the
first that meet its ear. Later, her lessons of anxious
care and fondest affection are the first that impress
themselves on its senses; it is she who explains the
beauties and wonders of creation to the awakening
intellect, the perfume of the bright red rose, from
which her fingers pluck the wounding thorn, the
sweetness of the grape or apple, the song of the
lark at early morning hour that wakes the tiny
sleeper; and, when the sun has disappeared in
the west, she points to the twinkling stars that
keep vigil above, while the little child learns to
lisp its innocent prayer of thanks and hopes, and
the curtains of night fall around the youthful
worshipper. But remember, my dear young
friends, that the mother cannot even then seek
repose; she watches and works; she must ply
the needle most busily, perhaps, during many
weary hours; and, while her hands are indefatigably employed, her mind is dwelling on the
needs and wants which the morrow has in store
for her loved ones; her heart aches when she
thinks of the possible shortcomings in the house-

hold, of a cold hearth and of empty shelves. And, if such is the daily round of the cares of affection and labours of love, when the blessings of health attend her family, what must be her intense sorrow when she sees her children suffer, what must be her agonising anxiety for their recovery, her despair, when the means appear insufficient to secure to the invalids every remedy, every cordial, every delicacy, the purest air, the most perfect quiet, and when she, poor mother, her whole heart rent with grief, and driving back the welling tears by the strongest effort of the will, can give only the most constant devotion, the most tender watching, the most gentle nursing, her hopes and her prayers! And the father, the bread-winner of the family, how he must toil, and struggle, and slave, that his little ones may have shelter, and fuel, and food, and raiment, how he must work at all seasons of the year and all hours of the day; and what endless, ever-recurring sacrifices of time, of rest, of sleep, of strength, of health, must he not make for his sons and daughters, from the moment they are vouchsafed to him by the blessing of Almighty God, from their birth until they leave the protecting roof to seek their own fortunes in the world—and far beyond that time ; for the love of parents towards their children is undying, more powerful, more glowing, more completely self-sacrificing, more entirely pure and unselfish than any other sentiment that ever dwells in the human breast!

Other feelings may become weakened, other loves may become fainter, and die away. The most indomitable love of books or glowing love of nature, the enthusiastic love of art or science, the most unconquerable love of travels and adventure, the ardent love of fame, the apparently insatiable love of power, the most eager and restless love of the world, the most concentrated love of solitude, the most impassioned hero-worship, the most intense and admiring love of friends, all may yield to circumstances, and be obliterated by them and by the effacing wing of time. But the love of father and mother for their children is everlasting. It is the latest human interest that occupies their thoughts ere they pass the mysterious boundary which separates this earth from the realms of eternity.

Children owe an indelible debt of gratitude, not only for the innumerable tangible gifts which they are constantly receiving, for the bread which the toiling father earns perhaps in the sweat of his brow, but also for the early lessons of life, for the training and the teaching, for the advice and the reproof, the encouragement, the solace, the recompense which are always theirs, and are incessantly yielded to them by love so pure, so boundless, so inexhaustible, so unchangeable, so enduring, that

it can be compared only to the endless love of the
Eternal towards all mankind. And probably it
is therefore that, when we call upon God and
implore His mercy, our language knows no name
more endearing and more beautiful than that of
our Heavenly Father.

We may indeed look upon our parents as the
messengers of the Lord, as the guardian and
ministering angels whom His bountiful wisdom
has placed near us. Father and mother are
possibly not free from faults and weaknesses, or
even from sin; but those blemishes and shortcomings, those imperfections from which none are
entirely exempt, and even those deeper stains, are
unknown to the children and unsuspected by them.
They see and feel only the depth and warmth of the
affection constantly evinced by fond parents; in
their eyes, and, in reality, with regard to
their little ones, the father and mother are
entirely blameless and pure. If pride, if vanity,
or better and nobler feelings, if a certain, yet
insufficient awe for the Divine laws and precepts of
religion, if respect for the opinion of the world, or
shame causes us to hide our faults from those
around us in general, how much more sedulously
do we veil and shroud them from the ever-in-
quisitive glances of our sons and daughters! And
though children may frequently be induced
to deem themselves superior to their parents,

cleverer, more highly gifted, better informed, and more accomplished — though they may be so in reality, and though anxious parents wish them to enjoy greater advantages of instruction and knowledge than have fallen to their own share: the father and mother still retain their position above them; for they possess the golden lessons of experience, and they are enabled to give those invaluable and daily lessons of love which guard the otherwise unprotected from infinite suffering and peril. And, therefore, my dear children, no one can ever replace our parents on earth. True and firm friends, good, tender, and compassionate men and women, may commiserate the orphans, and be kind to them, be they rich or poor. God alone is the Father of the fatherless.

But how may children honour those who gave them birth? How can they ever requite them for those inexhaustible treasures of love which have never failed them, but have lavishly supplied all their needs and wants? By un-murmuring, cheerful, conscientious obedience in childhood: for devoted parents wish to see their children good and happy; they know what will most surely promote their welfare, and they understand the development of the qualities and virtues which, under Providence, lead to goodness and happiness. Therefore the young will do well and wisely to submit to the dictates of their parents, to their guidance and their instruction, relinquishing their own fancies, and trusting to the sounder knowledge and judgment of those who love them with such unbounded affection. Later, when the mind becomes more matured, and the convictions assume a deeper, clearer, and more definite form, children will and should honour parents with every mark of respect and reverence, and prove to them as far as lies in their power that they are cognizant of a debt of deepest gratitude never to be entirely cancelled. Respect and reverence may be manifested in ten thousand ways, in matters of importance and in the trifling details of everyday life, by consulting the wishes of father and mother, and strenuously endeavouring to fulfil them, by avoiding contradiction and opposition, and by steering clear of every topic which might prove distasteful, and give rise to irritation or wounded susceptibility. For it is impossible to live many years without encountering obstacles and struggles, annoyances and disappointments, reverses and troubles, which leave either wounds, or sore and tender spots, or scars and furrows behind. A time may come when, in their onward journey through the mazes of life, parents will perhaps need help and support. Dutiful children should be the stay and the staff of their declining years, either by their bodily strength and activity, or by making every effort and straining every nerve to afford substantial assistance, to satisfy all wants, to keep away all cares from the honoured roof, and cause the light of serenity and contentment to shine around the sacred forms of those to whom they owe so much. But whatever duties of gratitude sons and daughters may be so fortunate as to fulfil for the comfort, satisfaction, and enjoyment of their parents, let these obligations be accomplished in all modesty and humility, not with murmurs and sighs as if they were hard and heavy tasks, but even if achieved by immense sacrifices, with all the rejoicing and gladness of devoted hearts; let them be laid on the altar of duty and love as a very trifling thank-offering for countless benefactions. But there is still another way, not included in the preceding, by which children may 'evince their thankfulness, —and remember, my dear young friends, that this is the best and highest recom-pense that father and mother ever anxiously wish, and ardently hope, and devoutly pray for on bended knees—namely, by a life dedicated to good deeds, to noble aims, to labours of charity, to works of merit and of zeal, and to the fervid adora-tion of our bountiful Father in heaven!

XI

RECREATION.

My dear young friends.

To you who are probably too much in-
clined to lay down book and pen, slate and pencil,
to children of tender years, and to all the very
youthful, who may, perhaps, look upon work as
wearisome, and who constantly yearn for the
cessation of it as a great enjoyment, who unconsciously deem learning and studying a troublesome
exception, and consider the absence of toil as the
only pleasant and most natural state of existence,
it may, indeed, seem superfluous to say that the
suspension of labour, the occasional, periodical, and
regular discontinuance of occupation is absolutely
requisite to recruit our powers, those of the body as
well as of the mind, in order to strengthen both, and
impart to them renewed vigour, buoyancy, and
freshness. The Almighty, in His infinite goodness, and in the marvellous fitness of all Divine
laws framed for our guidance, has graciously given
us the Sabbath as a day of rest, and you have
frequently been told how that sacred day should

be kept holy for meditation and especial prayer, for supplication and thankfulness, for a strict scrutiny of our past life, for wistful looks into a better future, for ardent longings that a more perfect achievement, a more complete fulfilment of duty may crown our efforts. But the grace of the Lord has given us many other days in the course of the year, many times of contemplation, which are both religious festivals and periods of rest and rejoicing. Repose, even in the secular sense of the word, is a necessity. He, who knows all our wants, has vouchsafed to us rest at the end of the week, not only that our thanksgivings may be offered to Him, the Divine Dispenser of all blessings and mercies, but also that we may be able to enjoy many pleasures provided by His endless bounty. Such is the Almighty's behest, as shown in the law of perpetual change, of frequent renewal and constant recurrence of all the same admirable phenomena. Everything in nature is eternally beautiful—the sky, the sun, the moon, and stars, the clouds, and even the storms followed by the rainbow of promise, the snow and the icicle, the flower and the tree, the lake, the stream, and the cascade. But how many changes pass over the lovely face of nature! and how tired should we grow even of its most enchanting attractions and most dazzling charms, were they always the same, ever fixed, unalterable, unvarying!

Should we rest satisfied, could we do so, even under
the vault of heaven, were it perpetually bright and
blue?　Glorious as is that sapphire dome, and
joyously as a fine day raises our hearts and
thoughts, and causes us to be more than humbly
and thankfully sensible of the goodness of the
Lord, and of the happiness of mere existence in
this world, we yet feel that the brilliancy of the
great orb should not be always unveiled, for we
know that the thirsty valleys of earth crave the
fertilising showers which do not flow from pure
azure spheres; we feel that the refulgent sun,
which sheds its splendour over woodland and
garden, and changes the green blades of the
furrow into golden harvests for rich and poor,
tinges the grapes of the vineyard with amber and
purple, and warms the peach of the orchard
into softness and sweetness, unfolds with its glowing breath the delicate petals of the rose, gives
colour and fragrance to every flower, and em-
bellishes alike with its beaming brightness the
palace and the cottage; we feel that this dazzling
and beneficent sun must not shine upon us uninterruptedly; its fiery rays would soon burn blossom and fruit, would devour the teeming pastures,
the fresh verdure of the earth, and drink and
drain all the welling streams of her bosom.　We
hail the crimson sunset, and with it the delightful
cool of the evening; we greet the fair moon

extending her silvery mantle over town and
country, filling both with her own fantastic and
mysterious loveliness, and transforming them into
realms of enchantment. But in that delightful
radiance we cannot tarry even one single night.
Beyond our protecting roof the heavy dews are
falling thickly, and resting coldly on the glimmering pavement or the emerald sward; and at
home, even the sheen of that pearly light cannot
prevent our weary eyelids from drooping and
closing, and shutting out its magic and gentle
splendour. And the clouds, with their ever fleeting and suggestive forms, speaking so powerfully
to the imagination, were they always hanging over
us, would they not dim and darken the earth
and our enjoyment of it, disturbing and threatening us with the storms which they bear in their
sable folds? It is true, these may sometimes be
lined or fringed with silver; but how much oftener
do they portend wind and hail, thunder and lightning! How frequently do they affright us, and
announce and work havoc and devastation ere they
can be dissolved, and replaced by that beauteous
and glittering bow, the heaven-spanning arch of
hope. You need not be told, my dear children,
that the ermine carpets of spotless snow which we
admire during the coldest winter season, and the
icicles which wreathe with diamonds the leafless
boughs of our trees, or spangle the lake and

petrify the cascade, would be beautiful no longer
if we thought they could chill and numb and
freeze for ever, under their hard brilliancy, the
bounding waters, the blooming meads, and all the
bright spots which minister to the delight, the
prosperity, and the happiness of the great family
of mankind.

Of the ever-revolving seasons, each bearing
its peculiar attributes, surrounded by its own
fascinations, bringing its own gifts and spells, how
weary we should grow if they did not appear and
vanish in rapid succession, lavish in blessings,
and fruitful and plentiful in enjoyments as they
doubtless are! Would the earth, over which they
pass, scattering their sweets and treasures around,
be so perfect and so beautiful, did not change
stimulate its forces, and develop them a thousand-
fold? And if this be the incontrovertible rule of
progress and of development in nature, can our
labour, the produce of intelligent hands, the work
of zealous minds or heartfelt convictions, be satisfactory to ourselves, and useful to others, if
monotony robs it of the energy, of the strength, of
the firmness required to bring it to perfection? It
is very true that perseverance, undaunted and
indefatigable, unflagging diligence, undisturbed
and uninterrupted attention are needed for the
satisfactory fulfilment of all obligations, for the
complete accomplishment of all duties. But, just

as our burdened and much-taxed bodily frame requires rest at the end of each day, and many hours of slumber, so our mind needs recreation, as a renewal of strength and elasticity. It seems necessary that our thoughts and endeavours should not always be directed towards the same objects, but that all our faculties be called into action, all our feelings roused, and all our intellectual powers unfolded, that many interests be allowed to claim our attention, and to engage a portion of our time and our efforts, so that we may not become entirely absorbed by our own more or less restricted circle of duties, and thus lose the satisfaction of appreciating that which is good and great beyond its narrow boundaries, forfeiting especially the unspeakable happiness of sympathising with others; it seems necessary that there should always, and under all circumstances, remain alive in us, not merely a faithful adherence, an ivy-like clinging to our own immediate round of obligations, praiseworthy and perhaps even admirable in its way, but also a warm and heartfelt desire to participate with the energies of our mind and soul in the busy life of the great external world.

And this, my dear children, is very different from the mere cessation of labour, from the mere habit of laying all implements of work on the shelf, from passing days in purposeless apathy, from giving up vacations to useless pastimes that can

leave no after-glow, no luminous track of experience on the mind or in the heart.

By recreation is meant renewal, renovation, progress, and improvement; not vacuity or emptiness,
but change of occupation. We cannot do wrong if
we consider recreation merely as a reward after
conscientious labour; then, alone, it will prove
refreshing and enjoyable; or if we look upon it as
a cordial to strengthen us for more strenuous and
long-continued exertions; but whenever we
turn to it, let us remember that it signifies not
listlessness, but the renovating effect of change, of
thought, and activity. My dear children, in order
fully to delight in the intermission of work and to
profit by it, we must occupy the eye, the ear, and
the limbs; we shall then feel, on returning to
the usual business of our existence, as if we had
plunged into vivifying waves, and shaken off the
dust, the cobwebs and the film, that must accu-
mulate if we plod on, in our own small nook—
it may be carefully, unremittingly, and merito-
riously—removed from the searching light of the
world. We possess, indeed, a faithful teacher in
the eye, so small in itself, yet so marvellously con-
structed, that, in the season of recreation, it can
roam far and wide, and reflect in its tiny crystal
mirror all the wonders and glories of earth, sea,
and sky, of towering mountains in their imposing
majesty, and smiling valleys, rich and bright with

the beauteous and exquisite produce of man's
industry, of the sweat of his brow, blessed by the
unfailing bounty and mercy of the Lord; it can
survey the attractions of the fathomless ocean, in
whose sapphire depths countless myriads of beings
live and die, unseen and unknown; the splendour
of the empyrean, with its incalculable millions of
distant suns, its flaming comets, unexplained
meteors, and mysterious shooting-stars.— And
how much does not the ear teach us! what
words, and what lessons—advice, warning, reproof,
pity and solace, comfort and encouragement, the
pleading, the prayers of the human voice, the
clear echoes of joy, or the sigh of sorrow, the
wail of suffering and of helplessness, the song of
gladness, the hymn of gratitude! How much may
we see and hear in hours of recreation, how
much may we learn, when, spell-bound by the
glowing pages of a fascinating book, we follow with
tears and with smiles the fortunes and vicissitudes, the trials and struggles of others! Or
how much may we find to admire when scanning
the varied leaves of the great volume of nature, not
merely while far away from home, and treading
the bridle-paths near glacier and precipice, over
which the chamois bounds and the eagle soars:
even a quiet walk along the hedge-row that borders
our village will show us the snowy and the crimson
hawthorn, the white blossom of the bramble, the

wild rose in its untended grace, all united by the
green ribbons of the bind-weed, and among this
exquisite sweetness and brightness the sparrow-
mother jealously guarding her new-born treasures.
In the dew-gemmed meadow, the lark is singing
her jubilant carols to the sun; but if we tarry
long enough in the balmy air, we shall hear the
nightingale pour out her soft ditties to the moon.

Let no one think that recreation is necessarily
frivolous or foolish; or, worse still, sinful and
irreligious. On the contrary, it ought, if well
chosen and regulated, to be much more than
perfectly innocent, it should lead to real improvement. To be cheerful and joyous can but tend
to raise our mental powers, and to give a fresh
impulse to our activity, which monotony might
depress and render torpid. It is even to be feared,
that if we deny ourselves every relaxation, and
adhere rigorously to our sphere of duty, however
excellent such a mode of life may be, we incur,
ere long, the risk of lapsing into indifference with
regard to all other aims and pursuits, of even
sinking into a mere mechanical observance of the
obligations of our calling, and certainly of allowing all important objects to fade away from our
horizon, except those upon which we are personally and constantly engaged. We thus lose
our highest privileges, and though our days may
be blameless, pure, and useful, our life will soon

lack some of its noblest aspirations; for we shall
cease to feel interested in our fellow-beings, cease
to cherish the sentiments, and to thrill with the
emotions, which lift us out of the groove of our
every-day career into a higher region of thought
and contemplation. Certainly, it is well that our
passage on earth should be marked by a life-long
devotion to duty, to those obligations which have
naturally devolved upon us; but let us beware of
becoming self-conscious, self-righteous, and narrow-
minded, of indulging in the belief that no path
can be good except the one we follow, whereas
there are many excellent, and perhaps better roads,
and let us refrain from supposing that relaxation can form no part of a useful and religious
life. There is no greater mistake, and most justly
and wisely has it been said that recreation is not
being idle, but easing the weariest part by change
of occupation. With the bright perspective of
needful change beaming in our mind's eye, well-
sustained exertion, and even hard work, though
taxing all our energies, will not weaken our
courage, nor damp our ardour; nor will pleasure,
if rightly understood, lead us astray, nor give us
a distaste for labour, which must ever be the first
condition of our existence. Quite the reverse—
the two equally balanced will lead to goodness
and to happiness, to the eager and joyful exercise
of the gentlest qualities and virtues, and we shall

find, that well-chosen recreation, a complete change in the spirit and heart of man, as over the spirit and face of nature, is carried out in accordance with the immutable and eternally beautiful law, and in obedience to the perfect and all-wise will of the Almighty.

XII.

"THE RICH AND POOR MUST MEET TOGETHER, THE LORD IS THE MAKER OF THEM ALL."

My dear children.

However faithful our memory may be, there are some truths that cannot be brought too often or too vividly before us, in order that firm belief in their importance, and full reliance upon their power, may sink deeply into our minds, be treasured by our hearts, and there remain impressed in ever-glowing and unchangeable characters. Among such truths I do not know any more cheering, more consoling, and more fortifying, than the beautiful verse, which tells us that the rich and the poor must meet together, for the Lord is the maker of them all.

We have been frequently reminded that, whatever our position on earth, before the throne of eternal wisdom, goodness and mercy, we are equal—equally cared for, equally beloved, equally pardoned, created alike in outward form, with the same wonderfully organised limbs, the same keen senses for the enjoyment of that world, which the Divine will has made so beautiful and so enchanting,

endowed with the same mental gifts and the same
immortal soul, sharing the same feelings, wants,
and wishes, hopes and fears, possessing and prizing
the same great treasures —the mother, who has
given us birth and life, and the first fond lessons
of tender affection, the father, who has taught
and indulged, or perhaps corrected us, the sister,
who has ever been our dearest companion, the
brother, who is our kindest friend; in later years,
perhaps, the husband or the wife with whom we
climb the hills or descend into the valleys of life,
and those most precious blessings, our dear children, the sons and daughters, who gladden our
eyes, whose youth is our second youth, whose joy
is our joy, whose happiness is our happiness, only
far brighter, purer and more perfect, because these
newly-awakened feelings are infinitely more free
from the alloy of selfishness, from the blemish of
egotistic longings, than those experienced by us in
our own earlier days.   And does not the same sun
warm us all—rich and poor?   Do not the same
stars glitter over our heads, a perpetual wonder
and mystery to our minds? Do not the same
winds fan the brow of the king and of the beggar?
Does not the same wheat-sheaf ripen for royal
banquets, for the loaf of the poor and the crust of
the mendicant ? Is there any guard of safety to
keep sickness and sorrow and death aloof from the
palaces of the mighty of the earth, any more than

from the homes of the poverty-stricken? Are
the great blessings of Divine Providence withheld
from the poorest, and are the wealthy removed
far above and beyond all trials, afflictions, and
calamities?

Surely not; there are, however, infinite varieties
of occupations, endless diversities of pursuits, innumerable differences of position. Some appear
to luxuriate in over-abundance, whilst others are
seen and known to eke out a scanty and wretched
subsistence. And yet the inequality is not so
great as it seems. You are aware, my dear
children, that a thatched roof shields us from the
scorching rays of the sun, from the descending
flood, from the winter's snow-storm, or the equi-
noctial gale, quite as effectually as the gilded
canopy protects those who dwell in marble palaces.
Our refreshing slumbers do not depend upon
downy couches; and the heart that beats under
the plainest garments may be as full of joy and
happiness as the breast that heaves under softest
velvets and finest laces ; the brow that knows no
ornament may be as free from care as that which
wears a crown, or sparkles with the light of
brilliant jewels.

So far as individuals are concerned, real felicity
does not depend upon riches and the pleasures
which they afford. A constant and perhaps
envious longing for these is just as sinful as it is

unwise, and even absurd. Yet, my dear children, let us also avoid the equally foolish notion that luxuries are valueless and superfluous. While it is perfectly true, that in thousands of cases they add but little to our personal enjoyment, it is impossible to deny the incalculable good they do by diffusing occupation and creating employment far and wide, multiplying labour, which is the salt of life, and stimulating industry, which supplies the necessaries of our existence. Our wants, which are perpetually and almost daily, and no doubt beneficently, increased by the progress of civilisation, by the gradual yet uninterrupted development of the latent forces of the earth, by the discovery and adaptation of their powers and uses—our wants and needs are found much simplified among the poor of other climes. We will not even glance at those still primitive and savage races, which support themselves entirely by fishing and hunting, and use the rudest implements to bring home for their sustenance the tenants of lake, and stream, and sea, or employ the coarsest weapons to snare and slay the birds of the air and the wild animals of field and forest. But there are many countries, where those who cultivate the earth, and assist in the produce and preparation of some of the treasures of commerce—as, for instance, the coolies from the great peninsula of India, who cross the sea to

work in the coffee plantations of the Island of
Ceylon—require marvellously little for their support and comfort. A shed extends over their
heads at night; otherwise their hours of rest are
unprotected by bolt or bar, by door or window.
The heavy tread of the wild elephant, roaming
through the native forests, does not wake those
weary sons of toil, nor does the prowling cheetah
disturb them; no pillow softens their slumbers;
they lie down on the bare bosom of the earth;
and, when they resume their labour at earliest
dawn, they have little to encumber them; they
require no luxurious clothing, not even sandals to
their feet; they satisfy their hunger with a few
grains of rice, and quench their thirst with water
from the fountain. This is merely alluded to, my
dear children, to prove that the farther we
are from the great seats of civilization, the fewer
are our wants; the nearer we are placed to the
chief marts of the world and to the centres of
wealth, the more our requirements increase, and,
as a rule, the better are we able to supply them.

It is one of the fundamental laws of eternal
wisdom and Divine beneficence that equality, with
regard to the chief needs of mankind, with regard to the great gifts and treasures which constitute happiness on earth, should pervade this
world and be the birthright of all; but it appears
as if, in every other respect, varieties of attain-

ments, diversities of talent and of rank, of avo-
cations, classes, and possessions, should continue,
and even increase a thousand-fold, until the end
of time. If all could be equally rich, or what is
called independent, consider, my dear children,
in what condition we should very soon find
ourselves.

You will easily see that the farmer would ere long
cease to till the land, and cease to supply us with
the produce of his labour, the gardener would not
prune the vine for the market, the miller would
not grind the corn, nor would the flour be kneaded
into bread for our daily meal. Each would have
to provide for his own selfish wants; not only
would there be no progress and no development,
the arts and sciences would soon disappear from the
face of the earth, and we should all imperceptibly
revert to the state of those hunting and fishing
barbarians, those savages, who are steadily reced-
ing before the onward movement of civilisation,
but who still inhabit some distant and benighted
portions of our globe.

Indeed, you will readily understand, that riches,
if they became general, would not exist long. Who
would go down into the bowels of the land, into
mines dark and deep, for coals and for iron, for
silver and for gold, or fell the trees of the forest
to build houses and ships, or work in quarries for
granite and marble, reap the harvest with heavy

scythe and sickle, press the grape, secure the vintage, or send with indefatigable fingers the shuttle across the loom?   A country, a nation, in order to be great and powerful, prosperous and happy, must be wealthy : a man or woman does not require riches to be happy and satisfied. Were it not so, life would be intolerable, both for those who lack the treasures of wealth, and for those who possess them.

Let us inquire of what elements happiness may be said to consist?   It is yielded most completely by tranquillity and cheerfulness of mind and heart ; it is evinced, though not always in the same manner, by the full and gleesome enjoyment of the passing hour.   So delightful a condition must be wrought by the consciousness of duty faithfully performed.   But fulfilment of duty is quite independent of riches, though these may, of course, prove useful for the accomplishment of our task.   Each of us has a mission, each a sphere of activity, where the best qualities and aptitudes find a fair field of action ; a circle not of unbending iron, but one so elastic, that, the greater our diligence and the greater our persevering industry, the more that magic ring extends, the wider it becomes, and the more claims it collects and brings under our notice for indefatigable exertion.

Divine Providence has decreed that all beings

may become useful, be their position high and great, or apparently insignificant and lowly; be it brilliant or modest; be they called upon to shine in the eyes of the world, or to plod and work on in some remote and obscure corner, known to the All-seeing, but unknown to their fellow-men; thus all may not only be happy themselves, but also hope to become sources of happiness to others. As in the universe created by Almighty wisdom, the smallest satellite, the palest and faintest moon, may be as necessary, and add to the general harmony of revolving worlds as much as the greatest stars and suns, so may, in the wide-spread family of mankind, the activity of the smallest and humblest be as useful as the works of the highest and mightiest. If, during many centuries, the little honey-bee distilled all the sweetness required for the consumption of man, if the silk-worm, even now, spins the most costly fabrics, if the tiny cochineal insect dyes the imperial mantles of the crowned monarchs of the earth, how much more can be achieved by human hands, and human lips, and human hearts?

The gladness derived from the fulfilment of duty is happiness; and this blessed feeling the rich and poor may share alike, for each has innumerable and ever-recurring obligations to fulfil. No pen could attempt to name all these duties, to point them all out for accomplishment. Let not the

poor be misled by the cares that oppress them
into the belief that the rich are unjustly favoured,
nor betrayed into bitterness of spirit and of feeling,
into that intense ill-will which annihilates brotherly
love. The wealthy may facilitate the task of their
less prosperous neighbour while remembering
that the Lord is the Creator of all mankind,
that He is the heavenly Father of all human
beings, that towards Him all should turn in the
hour of need and of plenty, of humiliation and of
triumph, of sorrow and of joy ; and let both the
rich and the poor always recollect that they can
serve Him only by serving their brethren, that
they can love Him only by loving those whom His
inexhaustible goodness has called into life. Not to
be wealthy is not a misfortune; that has been
abundantly shown and proved, as it cannot be
said to exclude the possession of the greatest, most
precious treasures, of those that can be neither
bought nor sold. But to be so poor as to lack
almost the necessaries of bare existence, must
indeed be a severe, a terrible trial; to feel the
sharp tooth of hunger, to feel it gnawing away the
bloom and health and strength of beloved children, more dear to us than life, not to have
sufficient raiment, sufficient fuel, sufficient shelter
for them, must be harrowing and excruciating.

Let us hope that such heartrending trials have
almost ceased to be realities. Not only have

individuals felt, but society at large has recognised, the sacred duty of providing for those who cannot provide for themselves. But while the wealthy must have a melancholy satisfaction in knowing that they aid the helpless, that they feed and clothe, warm and heal, teach and comfort the poor, those whom inevitable misfortunes, or vicissitudes, or even their own faults, have brought so low, let the needy remember and guard their own dignity, and strive by all means in their power to escape from the painful thraldom of almstaking.

Sudden attacks of illness, or long-abiding infirmities, unforeseen accidents, reverses not to be prevented by the utmost forethought may cripple the energies of the most industrious and hard-working, and crush the courage of the most hopeful. Often and quite unavoidably they change plenty into penury; but surely such are exceptions. As a rule, the wise husbanding of our resources, diligence, and persevering activity, thrift and economy, will keep us above want, will prevent poverty from being distressing, or galling, or humiliating.

And bear in mind, my dear children, that even the youngest of you can do much to lessen the general burden of poverty, by applying diligently to your duty, chiefly at school, during the early years of your life. The more knowledge there is, the less misery there will be throughout the world;

the more you know, the more means of success you will have, the more power to stem the tide of adversity, the more strength to overcome troubles and even disasters, the more ability to find useful and profitable employment, and to withstand peril and temptation. Fearful, for instance, as is the number of criminals sentenced to punishment every year, it is some consolation to find that more than one half of those committed are wholly un-educated, that they have erred and sinned from ignorance, or from idleness, which, even when compulsory, may become the parent of all vice.

Yes, the more knowledge there is, the more happiness there must be in the world; and the greater the wealth of the nations of the earth, the more resources individuals will find, and the more unlimited the demand for labour of every sort will prove to be. And thus it is in all phases of life. Arts and sciences, and all the profes-sions, manufactures, agriculture, and commerce crave for their development, for their extension, for their giant growth, the unceasing efforts of all who have learnt to work. The employers of capital must be also the employers of labour; human hands must tie the innumerable knots and meshes of the net-work of industry, which will, ere long, cover the entire surface of the globe. And thus the rich and the poor meet together, for the Lord is the Maker and the Benefactor of them

G

all. And as civilisation extends far and wide, those who have enjoyed the advantages of education and the pleasures of knowledge, will feel impelled to extend those blessings through all lands, to all classes, to all ages, in town and country.

This may appear a sanguine and exaggerated picture of universal prosperity towards which we are looking and labouring; all this may seem Utopian, and possibly there are some who, while hoping that such brilliant visions may be realised, murmur with sighs of doubt, "Alas! the poor exist; how can, and how should the rich meet them?" They meet them indeed, in earnest fulfilment of sacred duty, by the best gifts of kindness and benevolence in cases of distress and despondency, by giving, not only gold, but time, which is life; care, which is thought; the gentlest, clearest advice, and the brightest example, which may be called help; words of solace, which are like drops of balm to the bruised and wounded spirit; words of comfort to renew courage, which is hope and faith; and sympathy, which is tender fellow-feeling warm and deep. Thus we shall shield those who suffer, thus we shall surround them with the soft mantle of charity and brotherly love.

Yes, however limited our possessions, we may be rich; and justly can all those be called so who have and enjoy the treasures which their neighbours lack, be they health and strength and happiness, or merely patience and perseverance. And, while labouring faithfully with mind and body, heart and soul, let us look forward to that glad future of the human race, when the poor, being able to satisfy all their wants and needs, will harbour no sentiment of humiliation and dejection, and the rich need no longer blush at having left their duties unfulfilled, when indeed both may meet and thankfully and joyously acknowledge that they have felt and fathomed the beautiful truth of the words of holy writ, "The Lord is the Maker of them all."

XIII.

HEALTH.

"Remember thy Creator in the days of thy youth, ere the evil days come, and the years draw nigh, of which thou wilt say, I have no pleasure in them; ere the sun, and the light, and the moon, and the stars, are darkened, and the clouds return even after the rain."—Eccles. xii. 1, 2.

My DEAR CHILDREN.

Among the ever-widening circle of our duties, the one which recurs most frequently and reminds us most truly and unmistakeably of the extent of our obligations, of our greatest wants and needs, of our most keenly felt shortcomings, and which brings before us and defines most accurately our warmest wishes and fondest hopes, our most fervent longings and most arduous struggles, our endeavours, triumphs, and failures—that duty which calls imperatively for fulfilment at the earliest hour, when we open our eyes, and again at the latest, when we seek rest after the labours of the day, the duty of morning and evening prayer, is, among all nations of the world, in all countries, among all varieties of faith and creed, held to be the most solemn of institutions. It is

a duty performed by you, my dear children, long
before the true meaning of it can be fathomed
or deeply felt by your dawning intelligence and
awakening gratitude, a duty fulfilled in gentle
and loving obedience to the behest of fond parents
who taught your yet faltering lips to breathe
thanks to that all-merciful Father in Heaven, who
has given you to them, and who allows you to grow
and thrive to their delight and happiness. When
the earliest years of childhood have passed away,
and your own riper knowledge and the advice of
affectionate friends point out to your more
developed reason, to your more warmly thrilling
hearts, this great duty of thankfulness to the Divine
Giver of all blessings and mercies, it is difficult, nay, impossible to say, what shape your
thanks and supplications should assume before the
throne of the Eternal. Each of us holds in the
chambers of his soul the secret of his own weakness, of his own failings, of his own aspirations.
It may often be necessary to conceal from the
world, and even from our loved ones, much care
and anxiety, sorrow, suffering, and misfortune;
it may indeed happen that to strangers, to those
above and around us, our appeals, our requests,
and expectations appear ill-timed and exorbitant.
But in our humble communion with the Almighty,
all the words of contrition and of prayer, of fear
and of hope, of confession and of petition for

pardon, must be true and sincere. When seeking
the Divine presence, we can have no subterfuges,
no softening or obscuring veils, no exaggerations,
no mysteries, no secrets. Before the Fountain of
all indulgence there need be no concealment and
no reserve. His mercy we may always crave for
our hearts' desire ; He is never blind to our wants,
He is never deaf to our supplications ; and, while
we must always remain individually the best judges
of the prayer that each of us should offer to
Almighty God, there is one great gift, there is
one treasure beyond price for which you should
constantly pray at morn and eventide, my dear children, and yet never fear to be grasping or covetous.
I mean the first, greatest, and truest of blessings,
a blessing so perfect that it is, and must ever be,
our most valuable possession on earth ; a boon so
absolutely essential and so powerfully conducive
to the happiness of all human beings, so tran-
scendently precious, that the young and the old,
the poor and the rich, the beggar soliciting alms in
the crowded, busy thoroughfare, and the anointed
king on his exalted throne, are alike swayed
throughout life by its wondrous influence.

My dear children, that blessing is health ; and,
although to those who enjoy it, in half conscious
appreciation of its worth, the praise of its excellence
may appear a truism, the same words of praise
must seem poor and feeble and inadequate indeed

to those who have had the misfortune of losing
that marvellous gift, more precious by far than all
the gold of the earth and all the pearls of the
sea. Not only does it outshine every other gift
and enchantment with which the bountiful hand
of the Almighty has so lavishly adorned the
world, but without it nothing has any charm,
without it all is worthless. Bereft of health, we
are bereft of all : youth, mirth, joy, and happiness,
the freshness and sweetness of early spring, the
glow and brightness of summer, the calmer yet
still radiant beauty of autumn, the rosy dawn and
the brilliant sunrise, which silence the plaintive
nightingale, and bid the lark soar heavenward
with jubilant song, the fair moon with her
attendant train of bright-eyed stars, the fragrant
breeze, the rushing sea, the enamelled meadow
—these treasures and wonders are all as nought.
Our existence becomes one of suffering, and
those from whom health seems to be ebbing
slowly and painfully away, feel indeed helpless
and useless, a burden to themselves, a source
of constant sorrow and harassing anxiety to
others, to those perhaps most dearly beloved, a
cause of sadness dimming the light of the family
circle, casting a shadow over the day, deepening
the darkness of the night with fears and harrowing dreams, disturbing the time of rest which
should be refreshing, and weakening the day's

work which should be sustained and strengthened
by cheerfulness, filling with dullest care the hours
which ought to pass happily and merrily, clogging
those swift hours with heavy weights and irritating
shackles, hushing mirth, shattering energy, and
replacing the ever-changing aspect of joy around
them, and of contentment in their own hearts, by
the monotony of suffering, which too often, alas !
becomes the anguish of increased pain or the
overwhelming cloud of despair. You will say, my
dear children, that this is a melancholy picture of
sickness, suggested by sad and perhaps exceptional
experience, or conjured into existence by affrighted
imagination ; yet it falls short of the dread and
too frequent reality. We will not, however, dwell
upon it long. Let us look at it and think of
it, and turn away from its gloom to strengthen
an earnest resolve—that of working and toiling
and acting in grateful appreciation of that un-
equalled blessing, the disappearance of which
seems to annihilate all other mercies.

If health, in sunny days of prosperity, renders
our enjoyments more intense, if it adds a halo to
our truest and most perfect happiness, let us
remember that it is also a shield and a buckler,
a breast-plate and a spear, when difficulties and
misfortunes draw nigh ; that it enables us to
battle with temptations, and to vanquish obstacles ;
that it sustains our courage, gives us fortitude

to bear affliction, patience when we most require it, perseverance when we need that spur to ever-renewed exertion, and that alone it allows us to use activity and energy in the pursuit of our most cherished plans. Ought we not then, in humble thankfulness to the Almighty for the peerless treasure of health, guard it like the apple of our eye, with strenuous care, and with every pulsation of the heart, with every thought of the mind, with the work of our hands and the swiftness of our limbs, make the best and highest and noblest use of it, never abuse it, never deprive it of its lustre, never endanger it, so that it may never fail and never be lost by our own fault?

Let us then, my dear children, transform every hour of strength and energy into a period of positive, if not immediate satisfaction to ourselves, which must mean one of benefit to those whose well-being is bound up in our own. Believe me, health is the first and greatest of all earthly blessings ; all other gifts and powers are but feeble accessories : it may well be compared to the sun that gives light and warmth and brightness, that causes the leaf to expand, and the flower to bloom, the wheat to spring from the deep furrow, and the fruit to ripen on hedge and tree. It allows the limbs to grow and to be strengthened, the body and all its internal organs to acquire their full development, the brain to become the seat of useful and, perhaps, of great thought; it enables the life-blood in its rapid course to quicken all our actions, the heart to beat and thrill in unison with the mind for all good and noble purposes, for know-ledge and wisdom, for science and art, for justice and generosity, for devotion and self-sacrifice. Withdraw the light and warmth and brightness of the sun, and all becomes bleak and barren; the land does not yield its yellow sheaves, nor the vineyard its purple and amber clusters, the flower is nipped in the bud, the fruit chilled in the blossom. And so it is with health. Those who lack it, lack the power of action, the power of exertion. The germ of all goodness may lie in them, like the seed in the earth, the promise of all sweetness and beauty may be dormant in them; but there it remains, numbed by the icy touch of sickness, or withered by its fevered hand. Philo-sophers, and indeed all wise and experienced men of the world speak of the great and un-doubted value of time. But what is time without health ? No longer that swift-winged messenger of eternity which yields countless treasures to the active, the industrious, the indefatigable. No, shorn of its bright pinions, it becomes a heavy companion, extending a leaden canopy over weary heads, and thrusting sharp thorns into aching, and perhaps bleeding wounds. The

worldly and sagacious speak of golden opportunities: but what are these—even the most
tempting opportunities—with the promises which
they hold out of every advantage and enjoyment,
of success and fame, power and happiness, what are
they without health to profit by them? Nought but
delusive and tantalising sirens. Enthusiastic poets
sing, and thoughtful men in sober prose write of
the facilities and gifts and powers of the rosy morn
of life, of youth with all its witchery. But, alas!
what is it without health? A fitful and dis-
enchanting dream. And fatalists vaguely hint at,
and firmly believe in fortunate chances; but what
are they without the grasp of health to seize them
and convert them into springs of prosperity and
enjoyment? Mere illusions and delusions, created
to dazzle and deceive.

Thus, my dear children, you cannot fail to see
that the gift of health is the greatest of our
earthly possessions. Keep this belief in faithful
remembrance; keep it in the chambers of your
memory, not merely as a fact of useful knowledge,
but as a vital truth to be cherished and to be
acted upon, so that, ere you lay your head on
the pillow at night, you may ask yourselves in
perfect candour whether the great treasure, far
from remaining inert like wealth in the sombre
hiding places of the miser, has, at your earnest
bidding, been productive of good deeds or of useful

preparation for the future; whether you have prayed and worked, and fulfilled every duty of industry and of gratitude, of love and devotion, of purity and of zeal ; and whether you may lift up your hands to our Heavenly Father in earnest supplication for a renewal and continuance of the priceless gift which has enabled you to pass the day in useful labour, in true enjoyment of the blessings of life, and in humble and thankful adoration of Him, the bountiful Dispenser of countless mercies.

XIV.

SICKNESS.

"Trust in the Lord; be of good courage, and He will
strengthen thy heart, yea, trust in the Lord."

(Ps. xxvii. 14.)

" Into Thy hand I commit my spirit ; Thou redeemest
me, O Lord God of truth."—(Ps. xxxi. 6.)

MY DEAR 'CHILDREN.

Although we may watch and ward the
most precious of all our worldly treasures—the
blessing of health—and guard it with every power
of the body and the mind, keeping far aloof the
snares and the dangers that might imperil its
possession, and never allowing recklessness, folly,
vice, or sin, those most cruel enemies, to assail it,
never permitting those lawless offenders to break
into the stronghold, and carry off the prize—yet
health may elude the watchfulness of prudence,
the wariness of discretion, the self-command
and calm steadiness that would seem to surround and defend it like the outworks of an
impregnable fortress. Yes, the health of the most
robust is liable to give way, and illness may befall
the most prudent. This may appear suddenly, or

creep on gradually; it may be hereditary, or the
result of accident—no one is secure against it,
neither the young nor the old, nor the rich nor
the poor, nor the dull nor the clever, nor the
great nor the small.   Sore and heavy disease may
come on for a short period, or for many weary
years; it may be followed by gentle convalescence,
or be deepened into the most intense agony until
death closes the scene.   When the hand of sickness
smites us—whether we are sustained by buoyant
hope for renewed strength and energy, or weighed
down by the almost inevitable sadness and gloomy
prospect of parting from those we love and from
life, the chequered path of which has, nevertheless, given us enjoyment true and deep—
we remain chained by iron fetters, imprisoned
within the narrow boundaries of an arm-chair, or
laid low on a bed of torture, where all outward
independence, all bodily activity leaves us.   We
can no longer accomplish the daily work, which
is the salt of life; and this, my dear children,
applies equally to all sufferers on every step of
the social ladder.   There is an end to the exertions
of activity, to those occupations brought to us by
every dawning day, and to which we are wont to
look forward with eagerness for the benefit of
those who seem to depend upon our efforts.   There
is an end to our studies; the pen and the pencil
must alike remain idle; there seems to be an end

to all labours of love, and to the most precious of all—to the power of doing good.

In sickness, we may, and we involuntarily do, cause pain and sorrow to others; and we can no longer hope to contribute to their happiness. This is true, grievous, disheartening and irrefutable in its stern reality. It may well cloud the sunniest mind with dark and heavy shadows, extinguish the cheerfulness of the most sanguine, chill enthusiasm ardent and glowing, and freeze the fervid aspirations of the most courageous. But there are other equally irrefragable truths. Yes, there may be a cessation or suspension of our bodily independence; we cannot rush out into the school, where the first lessons of life are anxiously and sedulously taught, or into the college where, in noble rivalry with kindred minds, our intellect becomes matured and our talents are developed, where we may receive, or perhaps have the even greater satisfaction of imparting knowledge. We cannot seek the workshop or the labour-market, compete with those around us in the daily struggle for bread, for the bare necessaries, much less for the comforts and luxuries of life; or, if Divine Providence should have placed us in a different position, and fitted us for the acquisition of higher knowledge, of eminence in art and science, of fame and distinction in the world, we cannot even retain what has already been won—it glides away from our feeble and spasmodic grasp.

But even on a bed of sickness, we may teach and learn, we may yet possess and give—possess independence of thought, and give great and noble examples of fortitude. Between periods of suffering and during intervals of rest—for no pain, however slight or however severe, can possibly continue without intermission, as it would soon take us to the brink of the grave—we can form the determined resolve to bear the trials of bodily anguish with gentle patience, with humble resignation, and the perhaps still greater trials of utter prostration and helplessness, with the strength of mind that represses every sigh and curbs every movement of irritation, with that unwavering faith in the mercy of the Lord, which checks the rising murmur, silences repining, and assuages the bitterness of mental agony; we can endeavour to conceal, and thus actually mitigate painful thought, lighten the burden of those around us, and prevent our inflicting additional care and trouble upon sympathising hearts to whom our trials are already a cause of much sadness and sorrow. And then our sufferings will be robbed of half their poignancy, our recollections will lose their upbraiding bitterness, our prospects their sadness—and we may, with God's blessing, indulge happy dreams and bright visions of recovery —map out, as it were, a new life full of deeds of benevolence, of useful efforts, of well-directed

activity—learn to appreciate the great gift, which
is temporarily lost, the priceless treasure and its
intense enjoyments, which have been so fearfully
jeopardised—and we may gain time, the long
hours of the day, the sleepless hours of the night,
for grave thought uninfluenced by frivolous outward diversions, for candid self-examination uninterrupted by the more worldly duties which
claim our attention in health, for conscientious
meditation on the past, the present, and the
future, for a patient search into every corner of
the heart, that its weakness and its strength may
be discovered, that we may support the one,
and cause the other to yield good service. And
thus, while passive, or apparently so, we still offer
excellent and useful examples, and teach great
lessons never to be forgotten by those whom
affection, or friendship, or a sense of duty draws
towards us in our need. Constant patience,
unvarying gentleness, forbearance calm and firm,
and humble submission in pain and sickness, are
not mere words, they are great blessings, they are
heroic realities! We are well aware that some
sufferers, harassed by almost incessant pangs, or
by ever-returning anguish, are unable to keep the
tumultuous rising of their wounded and over-
excited feelings in subjection, and that while
half confessing these faults before the tribunal
of their own conscience, they nevertheless frame

an apology for impatience and irritability, un-
governable vehemence and irrepressible anger, by
pointing, not only to their overpowering woes
and torments, but to the entire annihilation of
consoling and counteracting enjoyment in their
existence.   It is very true that indulgent friendship and tender pity may easily excuse and forgive
the caprice and waywardness of those who have
so much to try their powers of endurance, while
perhaps not true friends, who painfully share all
afflictions, but kind visitors and faithful attend-
ants, though tearful and grieved near the bed of
sickness, may turn from the gloomy picture of
suffering to a bright circle of their own, where
content and happiness, the smiles of affection, and
laughter-loving voices may always be found.
Yet, believe me, my dear children, there can be
no greater mistake than to suppose that cares
and throes may justify any paroxysm of anger,
any ebullition of temper, any harshness of manner,
look, or word.   We shall suffer far less if, even
amidst agonising tortures or dull unremitting
woe, we can respect the feelings of others, and
learn to suffer unselfishly.   Though helpless
through sickness, we can help inflicting unneces-
sary trouble, and though apparently useless, we
shall be useful indeed if we can give a noble
example and teach others some of the highest and
most difficult tasks of life.   And remember, my

dear children, that trying as it is to be laid low
by sickness, it is infinitely more sad to see our
loved ones smitten by illness, sorrow and misfortune, to have anxiety gnawing at our hearts, and
grief filling the short span of our existence. Even
if death should threaten us, let us not indulge
merely in feelings of unavailing regret, keen
remorse and repentance, but may we cling
unweariedly to the performance of duty until the
last moment which we are destined to pass in this
valley of shadows and tears and trials. Our
courageous and strenuous efforts will and must
ever be the best preparation for crossing the
mysterious chasm which separates this world from
the realms of eternal peace and tranquillity
promised to weary and foot-sore sufferers on
earth by the loving-kindness and inexhaustible
mercy of our gracious Father in Heaven.

XV.

JACOB'S DREAM.

My dear children.

Not a day elapses without yielding to our enjoyment new blessings from the unbounded goodness of the Lord ; and though our ardent and heartfelt thanks are offered at the throne of mercy, there is not a single manifestation of Divine and constantly renewed loving-kindness for which we are, or ever can be, sufficiently grateful. He, the Bestower of all treasures, has gifts to brighten our earthly pilgrimage and to sweeten the cup of our life, to restore us after exhausting labour, to assuage our sorrow, to strengthen and sustain, calm and tranquillise, comfort and console us. Among these, let us, my dear young friends, think with heartfelt gratitude of the precious gift which is indeed more welcome to us than the long-prayed-for breeze to the becalmed ship in mid-ocean, more refreshing than the dew at early morn to bird and bee, more reviving than the same crystal drops at eventide to leaf and flower, more protecting than the shadow of softly waving foliage to the hot brow of the wanderer, more eagerly sought almost than bread by the hungry and starving, or than the bubbling fountain of the oasis amid burning sands by the camel and his rider. It is the great blessing of rest after the labours and anxieties of the day; it is the great mercy of repose for our weary limbs, perhaps for our weary hearts; it is that wondrous cordial which enables us to overcome fatigue, to be refreshed for the moil and toil of the day, to awake with a clearer view of surrounding difficulties, with a firmer resolve to vanquish them, with a brighter hope for the accomplishment of duty. It is the choicest balm for bleeding wounds, the best solace for the fainting soul; it is the great boon of sleep awarded to exhausted wayfarers on their road through life; and we are reminded of it when we read in the Holy Bible that Jacob "went out toward Haran... and he took of the stones of that place for his pillows and lay down to sleep."

He dreamed of a ladder set up on the earth, and the top of it reached to heaven. My dear children, Jacob, on waking, vowed to remain true during his whole existence to the worship of God, and, in those times of darkness and ignorance, when the earth was inhabited by barbarians and idolatrous tribes, that promise and Jacob's example were likely to effect much good. But,

in these days, my dear young friends, there is no
danger of our worshipping any other but the
Lord God, the Almighty, All-wise, All-merciful
Creator and Preserver of heaven and earth. There
is no danger of our doing homage to mere
wooden blocks or idols, who have eyes and see
not, ears and hear not, be those idols fashioned
out of clay, or carved in ivory, sculptured in
marble, or cast and chiselled in silver and gold.
We know the Lord our God, the only God of all
mankind, by the brilliant light of revelation, by
the laws and commandments graciously vouchsafed to us, by the chequered history of many
thousands of years; but not by all this alone do
we know God. His glory is daily, hourly, incessantly proclaimed to us by the greatness and
marvellous beauty of His works, by the unani-
mous voices of the whole creation, the grandeur,
the immensity, the endlessness of which our eyes
cannot compass, nor our minds comprehend.
The waters which gush in torrents from the
bosom of the earth, the mighty rivers, all teeming
with life, the great seas, sustaining in their mysterious, fathomless depths countless myriads of
organised beings, from the gigantic whale to the
tiny coral insect, the sombre forests, whose trees
grow to be, ere long, transmuted into fuel, or
changed into proudly careering vessels, the rich
harvests, nourishing all mankind, yet springing

from a few grains of seed dropped into the cold
ground, the joyous, carolling birds, the mighty
travelling winds, the dissolving clouds, the
dazzling sun by day, the illuminating moon by
night, the stars, those numberless distant worlds,
the whole sapphire vault of heaven, tell us of the
greatness and goodness of the Lord, and beautifully does David, the inspired poet and king,
exclaim in one of his sublimest Psalms: " The
heavens declare the glory of God, and the firma-
ment sheweth His handy-work. Day unto day
uttereth speech, and night unto night sheweth
knowledge." Therefore, my dear children, there
is no danger of our not knowing, of our not
worshipping the Lord. We all know God, and
many, nay all of us, strive to worship Him. But
let us guard against mere lip-worship—and may
we always try to remember that, however spacious
and bright our synagogues, they are but small
and dim in the sight of the Lord.

Marble pillars may be lofty, but how insignificant do they appear when compared to the
towering mountains that lift their snow-clad
peaks in grandeur and magnificence towards
the sky! Draperies may be gorgeous with many
colours, but do they rival the clouds o'er which
the setting sun casts his glowing treasures?
They may be richly woven, but do the most brilliant adornments equal the lovely flowers with

which the hand of God has embellished the green mantle of the earth ? And the clear flames of thousands of lamps—how dull and sombre they are contrasted with the ever-shining lights of heaven !

The universe, arrayed in a thousand unfading or ever-renewed beauties, is the temple of the Almighty, the whole creation worships and sancti-fies Him ; but for us human beings, endowed with reason and an immortal soul, it is not enough to build synagogues, and, on entering them, to join the choir of voices raised in glorifi-cation of the Lord, the source of all harmony. It is not enough to seek the house of God, Bible and Prayer Book in hand, on the holy Sabbath, and on great festivals; nor does it suffice in our own dwellings to read the sacred Scriptures, and to pray, however devoutly and fervently, at morning, noon, and night. Such supplications and thanksgivings, when flowing from pure lips, are, no doubt, acceptable to the Almighty, and become an additional blessing to ourselves by strengthening and sustaining us : yet they occupy, even in the existence of the most pious, but a small and inconsiderable portion of thought and time. Those who would really and truly and incessantly worship God should humbly but anxiously, strive to do so by their actions, by the unselfishness of their lives, by the faithful discharge of their duties, by severity towards themselves, by indulgence, charity, and kindness to others!

My dear children, the vision of Jacob's dream must ever appear a most admirable picture, a most soothing promise of Divine help; and in all lands, where the name of the Almighty is hallowed and His goodness adored, and during the centuries which have rolled by since that blessed dream shed its radiance over the patriarch's slumbers, how often has it not been thought and felt that many who lie down at night weary and footsore, lonely and friendless, in tears and in sorrow, and who have found or deemed the world a cold, hard stone, may, by the grace and blessing of God, be able to raise up for themselves a ladder resting on earth and reaching to the skies! That ladder is religion, whose hopes and consolations connect this world of shadows with heaven's own brightness, and the ascending and descending angels are the virtues which teach and help us to endure the cares, trials, struggles, and hardships of our earthly existence. The virtues are innumerable and well known, though perhaps not approachable by us all. You are very young, my dear children, and cannot be rich in experience; and while I pray that, whether you are dreaming or waking, the good angels of the Lord may always surround and befriend you, let me endeavour to unfold them to your view; that you

H

may remember and always zealously seek them
throughout life. You will try to keep nigh unto
them, so that gentle patience may teach you to
bear all vexations and annoyances, that indefatigable perseverance may assist you in over-
coming obstacles and difficulties, and that, in the
hour of sorrow, unflinching fortitude may lighten
the heavy burden of sufferings and afflictions.

Ardent hope and dauntless courage; charity
bountifully giving, and generously forgiving;
unwearied devotion, and self-sacrificing truth with
its torch of brightness, are all God's angels from
above descending the heavenly ladder to comfort
and strengthen us on earth. The angel of prayer
bearing the humble confession of our errors, bearing our ardent supplications, our fervid thanksgivings to the throne of Almighty God, travels
upwards on the mystic ladder, and when all is
dark and dreary on earth, the radiant angel of
faith points to that better land where wounds
do not bleed, where tears do not scald, where
there is no anguish for the mind, no agony for the
heart, but where peace is unbroken and happiness
undimmed.

XVI.

TIME FLIES.

My dear children.

The aged, and even those who are still climbing up the hill of life, and perhaps laboriously so, need not be reminded—for they know painfully well—how relentless time is in its flight. But to you, my dear young friends, it cannot be said too often that the great traveller has the most unflagging of all wings, and that neither wind, nor cloud, nor light, nor the rushing stream, nor the electric flash can fly along so rapidly or so unremittingly. The winds do not blow and rage perpetually; the fury of the tempest exhausts itself, and becomes hushed; the threatening cloud is, ere long, transformed into showers; even the light disappears, when to our eyes the sun sinks beneath the horizon; the electric flash accomplishes its work of usefulness or destruction, and expires; the wildly roaring stream leaps over boulders and rocks, and becomes absorbed in the waters of the calm river, or is taken up by the gigantic waves of the ocean. But time never tarries in its flight, it never rests, never stands still

—it careers on and on during millions and millions of years, while children grow and thrive and bloom, and men and women work and struggle, and succeed or fail, and fade and die, and sink into the grave, while whole generations disappear, and great empires 'become mightier and mightier, and decay and are blotted out, if not from the annals of history, from the maps of the world. Time flies indeed most swiftly, whether we seem to feel it glide gently and noiselessly by, or roll rapidly along; whether we become aware of its travelling onward and onward during the monotonous uniformity of our occupations, or note its progress when our duties are perpetually changing, and we pursue ever fresh and attractive studies; whether we move in an always varying round of obligations, or feel our life like a heavy chain, composed of thousands of links, to which an additional one is welded every day; whether our existence seems a garland of flowers, woven by our own fortunate hands, or we are watching with immense delight the germ, the growth, the expansion of every bud and blossom, the development of our labours, the fruition of our endeavours, the fulfilment of our hopes and wishes. We can never be oblivious of the flight of time; we are reminded of it, at all seasons of the year, when winter comes with its darkness and its frosts, when outward nature is cold and bare, when we seek shelter from

wind and sleet, when the fire blazes on the hearth,
and dispels the external gloom, when days and
nights appear alike long and dreary, or would seem
so, if we did not resolve to make good use of every
gleam of light, if we did not burn the midnight
oil, and sought to learn and to labour, when
nothing bright or beautiful calls us irresistibly
away from book or desk. But how soon winter
vanishes leaving our work perhaps half accomplished, how soon does it merge into spring, with
its blue-eyed violets and its songs of gleeful birds!
And that again how quickly does it unfold the
tender leaflets on every tree, how soon does it
hang its garlands on every hedge, cover every
orchard with its pearly and rosy clusters, spangle
every mead with its silver daisies, and waft sweet
incense throughout every bower! Oh! how pure
and fresh and soft spring looks, robing all the hills
with its delicate green, decking the earth with its
fragrant chaplets, and placing its nests with their
tiny broods in every shady nook! We wish it
might smile and last for ever. But it glides into
summer with its glowing roses, and ripening
sheaves, and its horn of plenty ; and then comes
autumn, with its sickle and scythe to mow and to
reap, and to garner up all the treasures of the
seasons. And thus years roll by, childhood with
its innocent pleasures, and youth with its warm
aspirations, and manhood and womanhood, with

their struggles and illusions, or joys and rewards, and then comes old age, with its infirmities. Let us hope that it does not come also with regret and self-reproaches, regret that all the light and warmth and sunshine, all the flowers have passed unheeded and unenjoyed, self-reproaches that nothing good, or great, or useful, has been achieved, and that life, the life that lies behind us in the shadowy past, is a dreary barren waste, without a brilliant oasis to look back to, and rest wearied and tearful eyes upon. Oh! could we but learn the value, the priceless value of every hour and its fleetness, the brevity of each golden morn, so cool, so quiet, so inviting for exertion after the repose of the night, the short span of the glorious noon, a type of that which our life should be in its fulness, with the warmth of our zeal for all good works, with the glow of our enthusiasm for all noble aims and thoughts, with the ardour of our devotion for all labours of love, the evanescent nature of evening with its softening shades, when the heat and the turmoil of the day are over, and we may indulge in earnest thought, and reflect whether the fulfilment of duty has been our great object, and if we have worthily attained thereto, and whether we dare hope that a pure conscience may indeed give us a good night, that period of complete rest when we recruit our strength to start again refreshed on the following

day, and recommence our efforts and endeavours.
Yes, every day, every week, every month, every
year brings its duties, and woe to those who
neglect the call. The opportunity of fulfilling
these obligations does not return, for time is
always on the wing. It never halts, never slackens
its speed, and waits for no one. Unlike thunder
which shakes the earth and ceases ; unlike ice that
melts, or snow that vanishes, or rain that is
absorbed; unlike the bird that seeks the branch
after having skimmed the fields of air, or the
joyous lark that cannot soar and sing for ever, or
the busy bee that at the close of day finds rest in
its waxen cell, or the fluttering insect that gleams
in the sunbeam, and then sleeps in the perfumed
calyx of the flower; the merry song, or the
gentle speech that pass away from the waves of
sound ; the smile that fades, the laughter that
rings no longer, the joy and the sorrow, the
hope and the fear, the love and the bitterness
that are alike quenched—unlike all these, time
flies on for ever and ever, and with it flies
our life. We cannot arrest the former, we
cannot retrace the steps of the latter. Then let
us make the best and wisest use of time ; to defer,
to postpone, to procrastinate, to leave the fulfilment of duty to the morrowing day, is a fault, for
which we can never atone. It may be a sin.
Who knows, my dear children, to what mischief

or misfortune, to what sadness and sorrow procrastination may lead ? If you, as helpless little
infants, had been confided to our care, could we
neglect you during only one short day, neglect to
clothe and feed you, neglect to screen you from
cold, and not risk and imperil your very existence? And later, when your own responsibilities begin, when you, though still early in life,
when you, though still tenderly watched, have
already acquired some personal volition and
control over your actions, when the circle of your
obligations becomes perpetually larger, bodily,
mentally, and morally, can there be an excuse
for your trusting to the morrowing day? Ought
you not, during the precious years of childhood,
to observe, listen, and study? should you not try
with all your power and energy to learn all the
great lessons which cannot be acquired and taken
to heart too soon, and remembering especially the
many aches and ills to which flesh is heir, the
sickness that may overtake us and lay us low,
or harder still, the dire disease that may smite
our loved ones, the inevitable interruptions that
occur unexpectedly, and cannot be warded off, the
great afflictions and the minor cares and annoyances, should you, should we not endeavour early
and late to learn unwearied patience, energetic
perseverance and unflagging industry, so as to
overcome slowness of apprehension, and not to

be rebuked by it, to conquer difficulty of execution, correct defective memory, rob heaviness of its
chains, and arrest light-footed heedlessness? It
may run away with our best intentions, and lead,
ere long, to an utter and a dangerous want of
thought and care. And remember, my dear
children, how comparatively easy it is in early
years to uproot faults and check evil tendencies.
The latter have not become so wild and uncontrollable as not to yield to the restraining but not
wounding effect of silken strings and guiding
reins, and the former may assuredly be subdued
if we always keep in mind that time flies, that
delay is a self-inflicted peril and wrong, and that,
in childhood and youth, when we still possess the
anxious watchfulness of loving parents to remind
us of our duties, to warn us against every neglect
of our task, it is easy to reward and delight their
affection by showing cheerful and ready obedience
to their hearts' desire. How much more difficult it
is, later in life, when conscience often blunted by
self-indulgence becomes our only guide, when habit
has perhaps confirmed our weakness and waywardness, when indolence or apathy binds us with its
fetters, when the voice of teachers is mute, when
true friends are far away, and cannot bid us
hearken to the call of duty—how much more
difficult is it then to remember that time hurries
relentlessly on—how easy, how fatally easy to

waste precious hours, to let golden opportunities
for self-improvement, for devotion glide by, and to
leave the fruit of the tree of knowledge untasted.
Do not speak of the morrow—it brings other
duties, other cares, and lost time is indeed a
priceless treasure, an invaluable jewel, as irretrievably forfeited as if it had been buried in
the depths of the ocean. By tardiness we wrong
ourselves and others. Delay, ever recurring delay
during the early years of life, a mere thoughtless
postponement of lessons to be learnt, of studies to
be pursued, deprives us of an inexhaustible mine
of wealth, of an ever-blooming paradise of enjoyments. Who can tell how much knowledge we
might otherwise have acquired, how many tastes
we might have cultivated and developed, which
would have endowed us with the best resources,
and proved fountains of delight to others, how
many talents we might have unfolded to embellish
our own life, and lives dearer to us than our own!
Remember, my dear children, that each little
spray of beauty and sweetness which we may gather
for ourselves from the echoes of song or realms
of poetry, from the enchanting loveliness which
pervades this world, that each gift helps to
brighten hours of dulness, to tide over long periods
of trial and suffering! But we can tell, and we
know, that procrastination nips all hopes in the
bud, and clouds all radiant promises of the future,

inevitably flinging between us and every brilliant perspective the shadow of an unsatisfactory past, of duties unfulfilled, of pledges unredeemed, of neglected obligations, of work uncommenced, of obstacles unsurmounted. For remember, my dear children, that time is not ours, but that we must obey its behest.

If all this applies to our childhood and the earlier years of our life, when the circle of our duties is plainly and indubitably marked out, and we still have a monitor by our side, how much more forcibly does it apply later, when the way has been smoothed, and the rough and hard work of education is accomplished, when our powers of reasoning are more acute, our feelings warmer, and no longer the mere fleeting emotions of childhood, when our longings are more intense, our aspirations more fervid, when all our sentiments are quickened, when our will is so much more tenacious, when our wishes are more ardent, our prayers, if not more true and heartfelt than in childhood, more earnest and definite, when we know what is right, not merely from the lips of our teachers, from the pages of our books, but know it already from the lessons of experience, that sternest and severest, if not best of instructors, know it with all the strength and power of heart and soul and mind. Then indeed delay, if indulged in, inevitably draws a sombre veil over much that might otherwise be sunny; then it may become worse than a fault, for it often deepens into sin. We wish to act justly, to be truthful, liberal and charitable; we may have frequent opportunities of proving our generosity and devotedness, we may have less frequent, but still great calls upon our self-denial and self-sacrifice. Without any special reason for delay, on the contrary, with every possible reason and inducement for exertion, but merely from the foolish and fatal habit of postponing every thing to the morrowing day —we procrastinate. The activity which is intended to ward off embarrassments is too long thought of, too long deferred; the labour of love, which demands the efforts of indefatigable hands, is commenced too late; the act of justice is accomplished too tardily to shield from obloquy and misery; the liberality that would have helped to dispel fanaticism and bigotry, or to annihilate prejudice, comes too late; the generosity intended to cheer and reinstate, the charity held out to help and save, all are too late; the devotion, the self-sacrifice, the self-denial are useless, they come too late, alas! when those, whom our exertions and endeavours were to benefit, are perhaps removed beyond human power and influence. Probably you will think, my dear children, that an exaggerated picture has been drawn, and that a fault apparently so trifling and so venial as procrastination could not possibly lead to such grave and sad results, to ignorance and sloth, to a dreary waste of opportunities and of life, to idleness, to the neglect of duty, to endless upbraiding, perhaps to unceasing remorse, to the destruction of happiness, to misery seemingly unmerited and to unexplained misfortune.

It has justly been said, that it never can be too late to mend. Yes, provided we begin the work immediately, and do not postpone every step, defer every effort, and make the commencement too tardily. But we can not delude ourselves; the effort must be great—as, by years of apathy, our best faculties have probably been weakened, our strength has become undermined, our firmness shattered, and our energy impaired. To eradicate these faults, which delay has engendered, it is, alas! difficult, and perhaps even too late; to pluck out indolence, and remove weakness and vacillation, may be the labour of a giant, for time is ever and relentlessly on the wing—hurrying us on to that mysterious doom where all exertions on this side of the grave must inevitably cease. It has been remarked, that to be always intending to lead a new life, but never to begin it, is as if a man should defer eating and drinking and sleeping from day to day, and night to night, till he is starved and destroyed. My dear children, do not destroy yourselves mentally and morally by starving your minds and souls,—it is a grievous sin. Keep your intellect fresh and bright, by admitting into its recesses every generous idea, by cultivating every noble thought, that your labours may yield still nobler fruit—and feed the life-stream of your hearts with every feeling, deep and warm and true, that may call forth works of real excellence—such works as we are commanded to accomplish, in order that we may not pass an unprofitable, purposeless existence, nor appear empty-handed before the throne of eternal justice.

XVII.

TOLERATION.

My dear children.

All honestly conscientious workers in the great and wide field of life must have the same objects in view, and in their anxious and heartfelt endeavours, cherish the same final purposes—they can wish for nought but the recognition of truth, the extension of virtue, the diffusion of knowledge, of prosperity, and happiness. All religious exercises and convictions have but one goal—internal peace; they have been beneficently designed to help and uphold us, to strengthen our weakness, and to change it into power for the fulfilment of the arduous duties and the accomplishment of the difficult obligations of our career; they have been wisely framed to sustain our courage on earth; and give us bright-winged hopes to carry us beyond the confines of this world. But it would almost seem as if, among the many millions who inhabit this globe, not two, equally eager and zealous wayfarers, could—though their object be identical—follow the same road, the paths being indeed innumerable which lead from earth to heaven. Such paths, often laboriously carved out of difficulties, are, or appear, multifarious, because the innate gifts, as well as the acquired attainments of the travellers, are infinitely varied, and become still more strangely modified by circumstances and opportunities.

It may perhaps be thought that there cannot possibly be any injustice in setting up a high standard of morality for all around us, and, in speaking of the deeds and actions of others with stern and rigorous severity, because there is only one golden rule of conduct, true and perfect, one balance of good and evil, one law of morality and virtue for all. To a certain degree this is undoubtedly the case; and we may indeed expect a fulfilment of duty from every member of the immense human family; but beyond that line, which must ever vary and change according to events and incidents, situations and conditions, indulgence, gentle, thoughtful and considerate, becomes an obligation; for we hardly suspect the difficulties, which even those nearest to us have to overcome in the daily endeavour of doing right and shunning wrong: some halt in sad perplexity before obstacles, which appear mountains to them, but remain perfectly unknown to others; many among us are urged on, by the might and power of circumstances, to the accomplishment of all deeds of usefulness and excellence, while circumstances equally powerful and imperative may keep others aloof. Let us, therefore, be tolerant of the most evident short-comings, of faults of omission, of apparent though often hardly real remissness, and also of real, but undeserved failure.

And if diversities in the fulfilment, or seeming neglect of the duties of every day life, crave our forbearance and demand our most lenient construction, how infinitely more tender and careful and tolerant should we be in the almost boundless domain of thoughts, opinions, and convictions? Are they not the joint produce of peculiarities, of mental organisation, of the sedulous training of these qualifications at home, or of their development at school and college? In the former case, it would be difficult, if not impossible, to uproot such individualities; for in that intricate labyrinth called the human mind, they may probably be necessities; while in the latter, they are the vivid and indelible impressions made by earnest teaching on early childhood and ardent youth, and such impressions are apt to exercise an incalculable sway over the whole extent of life. But, even were it possible to change our views and opinions so as to assimilate them to those of our friends, or could we alter the views and convictions of the surrounding multitudes or individuals in order to make them resemble our own, and agree with them completely, it is very far from evident, that either the troublesome and laborious process of change, or the result of transformation, would be desirable; while experience shows that so difficult a task is seldom successful, as it might lead, unfortunately, and not unfrequently, either to hypocrisy or to indifference—misfortunes far greater and more deplorable than even a glaring error of judgment, which can never be criminal or sinful.

This becomes especially clear when we endeavour to make the application of it in the realms of religious belief, to which the words intolerance and toleration, and their meaning, have usually, but not justly, been confined. Children receive their religious creed at the hands of their parents; they share the faith of father and mother, whose earliest lessons teach them to adore the unseen Benefactor of all mankind, the Creator of heaven and earth, of all their ever-varying beauties and unchanging glories. And this belief, which children owe to their parents, comes, so to say, naturally to them, harmonising with the love and reverence they feel for the father, who is the visible and earthly symbol of the invisible Preserver, of the great Bestower of all gifts, of the omnipotent Dispenser of all blessings, of the merciful Pardoner of all offences. Religious feelings thus called into glowing life, cannot be otherwise than ennobling, beneficial, and conducive to happiness. To relinquish the principles, the tenets and convictions we have thus early imbibed and learned to cherish, to abandon them lightly, and perhaps from mere worldly motives, cannot be otherwise than dangerous, and appears especially wrong when, by such a fearful rent, the tearing asunder of all the sacred ties which bind us to loving parents is contemplated. And, therefore, my dear children, all attempts at making proselytes is emphatically forbidden by the Jewish religion, which, in the fullest reliance upon the inexhaustible goodness of the Lord, teaches us to believe that the pious and virtuous, the really good, pure and single-minded of all nations, all centuries, and all shades of faith, may hope to win eternal felicity in the realms of everlasting bliss. Yes, my dear children, such attempts are peremptorily interdicted by our sacred religion, which trusts to the power of the immutable truths enshrined in its holy and inspired teaching, to convince and to win others, without the imperfect agency of human words or efforts.

Should, however, our form of belief rest not upon lessons imbibed in early childhood from affectionate and watchful parents, or later, though still in early youth, from devoted and most justly revered masters, but be the result of free choice and of the truest and deepest conviction, then it must surely be the offspring of all the inmost powers

and characteristics of our nature. Conscientiously
evolved out of the depths of heart and soul, it
leads us on to the sincere love of our neighbour, to
the zealous accomplishment of duty, and enforces
humble and pious submission to the decrees of
Divine Providence. This great and goodly harvest,
however, can be matured and reaped only when
the faith, whose produce it is, responds to the
internal and external experience of life, satisfies
all our eager and inmost cravings for anchors of
safety and havens of spiritual rest, all the ardent
longings of our breast for light and truth and peace.

Who shall say whether our creed can fulfil all
those conditions? We alone, in the deepest
chambers of our hearts, are able to answer this
all-important question. Religion has been vouchsafed by Divine grace to enable us to understand
the great lessons of heaven, and act in anxious
obedience to them on earth. But not all eyes see
alike, and each may need a different lens to discern
the wondrous stars of the empyrean. We know
that in many respects our own opinions and convictions often yield to the irrefutable teaching of
experience; why should we deny to others the
toleration which we so very often have occasion
to crave at their hands, and which we frequently,
nay, constantly, exercise towards ourselves? Can
a new light in our path distort our view of duty,
or make us oblivious of it? On the contrary;

every new flame kindled in our heart points out
all our obligations more clearly, and causes us to
feel more anxious to persevere in every good work.
Then why should we have less faith in the moral
power of others? Why should we not deem
them deserving of friendship and regard, esteem,
respect, attachment, or perhaps reverence and
admiration, merely because their opinions and
convictions on a few, or even on many subjects,
do not coincide with ours? Surely, no one would
yield to feelings otherwise than tolerant, if the
terrible calamities evoked by the fierce spirit of
persecution, could always be kept, not merely in
vivid, but in glaring and alarming recollection.
We shudder when history unfolds her blood-
stained annals, and, with warning finger, points
out to posterity the fearful crimes, the fiendlike
atrocities, committed in the sacred name of religion, and when we remember that the most
unrelenting cruelties, the most iniquitous tortures, the most ruthless murders, the most bar-
barous executions were planned and inflicted by
wild fanatics, whose blasphemous tongue dared to
invoke the Almighty's help and blessing upon
heinous deeds of darkness and extirpation, as if
the All-merciful could find pleasure and satisfaction in anything but that which is good and
righteous, loveable and beautiful — He, who
allows the heathens and their mighty empires to

exist, and even to flourish, if, in accordance with their knowledge of right and wrong, they shun the latter and practise the former. It may be said, and with perfect truth, that the progress of civilisation protects us against the recurrence of such fearful errors, against such guilty aberrations, and that in the broad light of the present day, persecution and oppression on account of religious opinions, are unknown; that, in the most enlightened countries, even political and social disabilities are being abrogated by law, or are fast disappearing by tacit and general consent. This is a true blessing, yet even this is hardly sufficient; so long as any dislike, not to say antipathy, separates us in the depths of the heart and conscience from our neighbours, merely on the untenable grounds of difference of belief—we cannot know and appreciate the full meaning of toleration; we cannot love our neighbour; we cannot fulfil towards him all the duties of brotherhood; religion, whose sublime mission it is to connect all mankind in bonds of affection, will isolate us, instead of leading us in friendship and devotion towards those whom it ought to be our privilege and our happiness to help and to cherish. The great work of our self-education will not be complete, my dear children, until we can look upon every form of thought, creed and faith—not with coldness and indifference, but with that true respect for, and genuine sympathy with sincere belief, which must exclude all anger, bitterness, and irritation; until we can live and act in gentle harmony with one another; for it is by such brotherly endeavours, by such union, that we may hope to transform good and great aims into noble realities.

The objection most frequently raised against the soothing and comforting theory of the universality of God's all-embracing love and mercy, seems to be that there can exist but one unchanging, unchangeable and eternal truth, that whatever may have sprung up beside and around that brilliant, all-illuminating light and warming flame, must be wrong and deluding, a will-of-the-wisp, an *ignis-fatuus,* to entice men away from the broad royal road.

My dear children, we cannot prize our own sacred and beauteous faith too highly, we can never value it enough. Let us cherish it with all the powers of heart and soul graciously implanted in us by the paternal hand of our beneficent Creator and Preserver; it is indeed the most precious gift vouchsafed by His goodness, a diamond without a flaw, of perfect and matchless purity—a column of fire so brilliant that before its brightness all dark shadows disappear, all veils fall to the ground, all mysteries vanish.

It has provided rules and laws for all times

and all seasons, for all nations and all countries; inexhaustible treasures of knowledge and wisdom for all minds, ever-flowing sources of joy and of hope, of balm and comfort, solace and strength for all hearts; it has proclaimed the unity and the worship of the Almighty throughout every portion of the globe, filling all countries with the adoration of His Divine name. Can the Decalogue, the law of every civilised land, ever be surpassed or abrogated? Is not the Book of Proverbs an inexhaustible mine of deep thought and golden wisdom ? the Book of Psalms, the most marvellous expression of every feeling and emotion that can agitate or soothe the human breast—of ardent longings, bright-winged hopes, sublime aspirations, glowing faith, radiant happiness, profound gratitude and fervid adoration of the Eternal, of gentlest sorrow and unmurmuring affliction, of weeping without bitterness and mourning without despair ? The Divine harmonies of the Psalter console and cheer the struggling and the suffering, the living and the dying, and its immortal melodies will float and ring and sound with blended power and sweetness through all centuries to the end of time !

But it must surely have occurred to thousands among us that in this great and wondrous world, where nothing is the work of chance, so many varieties in the worship of the All-High could

not possibly exist, unless, for some wise purpose,
unknown to us, He had allowed and decreed this
endless diversity in the mode of adoring His everlasting and unbounded goodness and greatness.
Every way of devoutly acknowledging and piously
appreciating Almighty God's omniscience, omni-
potence, and omnipresence, seems to be a new
manifestation of His power. The sun lights and
warms the whole earth ; but does it bring forth
the same productions in all zones and climes ?
does it not kindle into life, and develop into
beauty and usefulness, for the enjoyment of man,
a boundless profusion of gifts in every quarter of
the world ; and even in the same latitude, on
infinite varieties of land, in the crystalline depths
of the waters, or azure fields of the air, does
it not yield endless diversities of blessings to
satisfy our wants, to supply us with luxuries, or
to charm our eyes with ever-renewed delight?
The tea-shrub and the hop-plant, the sugar-cane
and the vine, cotton, wheat and oil, the fever-
subduing bark and the pain-allaying poppy-juice,
the freshness of every fruit that ripens, the perfume of every flower that blooms, and each blade
of grass that grows, are they not, one and all,
emanations of the Almighty's infinite goodness?
And if the countless gifts of His beneficence are
so manifold and so rich, adapted to the wants and
tastes of all men in all lands and times and

I

conditions, why should not the expressions of our gratitude be permitted to vary according to our perceptions and to our powers of utterance ? Why should not, for some great purpose hidden from our limited vision, every form of true and heart-felt worship be ordained by Him and find favour in His all-seeing and all-searching eyes ?

XVIII.

CLEANLINESS.

My dear children.

While reflecting on the importance of our obligations, while hoping and endeavouring to fulfil them to the best of our abilities, it would be difficult, if not impossible, to fix the order of precedence among duties. Though some are of greater urgency and importance than others, the estimate we form of them is much and indeed endlessly modified by the great variety of thought and feeling inherent in human nature. The easy accomplishment of many of our highest duties may perhaps be the spontaneous response to an inborn craving of our hearts, the ready answer to a natural longing, yielded so easily by our inmost soul as not to make any effort or sustained exertion requisite for even the most unceasing labour of love; while other tasks, not congenial to our inclination, seem to demand a great and constant struggle, an indefatigable wrestling with our reluctance, with our stubborn dislike, and our own dangerous and often fatal weakness.

Still, if called upon to define our duties, independently of any personal considerations, we might probably point out the greatest of them with readiness. Yet remember, my dear children, that even the smallest and apparently the least important, those which seem to belong to our worldly welfare only and to the humble occupations of daily life, are nevertheless indissolubly connected with the greatest truths, with the highest consolations of our holy religion. While our first duties must ever be those of tender mercy, gentle forgiveness, unbounded benevolence, unflinching devotion, and unrepining self-sacrifice, your attention, my dear children, will to-day be called to the seemingly humble and lowly obligation of cleanliness.

You will easily understand that in order to be merciful we must cleanse ourselves from all harshness; to forgive offences softly, and to forget injuries completely, we must wash out every stain of anger, and remove every drop of bitterness; to practise unbounded benevolence we must purify ourselves from selfishness; to be devoted and ready for every sacrifice, we must sweep away from the breast all impediments, all obscuring mists, so that the path of duty may lie in shining clearness before us, and beckon to us steadfastly and fearlessly to tread its heights and dive into its depths. We shall not find this task of purifica-

tion above our strength if we invoke the blessing
and help of the Almighty, and if we recollect
that as the fresh breeze of morning enters into
the casement, and drives the heavy atmosphere of
night away, so the spirit of God will chase away
from the oppressed, the weary and the listless
soul, the dreary inertness, the clouds of heaviness, which render it incapable of noble aspirations and deeds of excellence. We shall not be
daunted in our endeavours if we remember that
as the fragrant air, laden with the balmy breath
of morning, is to the close, fever-haunted room,
driving darkness and danger away, and filling it
with sweetness, so is the reviving, invigorating
inspiration from the heavenly throne when it
discloses to us the higher view and nobler aspects
of life —when it penetrates into the recesses of
the human heart, so replete, alas! with petty
prejudices and conceits, little aims and vanities,
small whims and follies.

My dear children, whenever we read the Bible
attentively, we shall find therein a marvellous
combination of all duties. Those which appear
as if they might have been dictated by common
sense for purposes of health, are nevertheless
closely linked to the duties of religious zeal, and
the ablutions prescribed to us are nearly allied to
the great laws of purity which ought to rule our
whole existence. The knowledge of this truth

should encourage you, my dear children, to persevere, and should increase your pleasure in
striving to give, in faithful obedience to the
Divine behest, even to the poorest home, the first
of all necessaries, the greatest of all comforts, the
most enjoyable of all luxuries—cleanliness; which
frequently wards off that dread fiend—disease,
and promotes the greatest of all blessings—health.
Palaces may be gorgeous and dazzling, but surely
they are not pleasanter to look upon than the
dwellings of industry, bright with comfort and
cleanliness. Who does not like to see the spotless
floor; the well swept hearth, warm with the glow
that sheds the brilliancy of its enlivening flames
all around; the household vessels of tin and
pewter shining like silver; the brass candlesticks,
the Sabbath lamp, sparkling like gold; the glasses
on the dresser, glittering like jewels; and windows, not dim with the spider's web, but though
small, brightly clear, and letting in the light of
heaven, to illuminate a happy group of parents
and children, brothers and sisters, and loving
kindred, forming a picture of health and cleanliness, of industry and contentment?

My dear young friends, only the carelessness,
only the slovenly habits of man have obscured and
darkened much that we see around us in black,
narrow streets, and dingy lanes, and gloomy
courts. In nature, in the beautiful works of

Almighty God, all is clean, and clear, and bright, and pure — the rain that drops from the clouds to wash, and cleanse, and fertilize the land, the dew, both at rosy morn and glowing eve, the snow, that forms a dazzling ermine mantle for the earth; even hail, destructive as it is, falls down in showers of pearls and diamonds; and mists are white like bridal veils. The mountain-torrent is pure as crystal; the lake is transparent, the finny tribes that live in its waters are covered with gleaming scales of ruby and gold; the birds of heaven—the robin with its flaming breast, the swallow with her silken plumage—flitting from branch to branch, or floating through the clear atmosphere, look beautifully bright.

My dear children, let us ever strive after cleanliness in our dwellings; after still greater cleanliness in our personal appearance; and be our outward garb an indication and emblem of the purity within, of a pure mind, a clear conscience, a spotless heart. During the wear and tear of a long life, the inward cleanliness may become overcast and obscured by specks and spots. Let us ever, my dear children, hasten to remove them by repentance, by contrition, by atonement, that these defects may not deepen into indelible stains; and, as we wish to keep our homes free from uncleanliness, even so let us strive, but still more anxiously, more incessantly,

and more strenuously, to keep our immortal soul
aloof from all taint and impurity, so that after a
long career of toils and trials, we may be able, at
the hour of death, to consign it, in all purity,
to our guardian angel, that it may be borne on
wings of light to the throne of Almighty God.

XIX.

PRIDE AND VANITY.

My dear children.

Any one of the numerous faults to which weak and often erring humanity is prone, has so many roots and rootlets in the depths of the heart, so many branches and sprays in the mind, sends out so many limbs and offshoots, that it may well require our most strenuous care, our unremitting attention to destroy it; and claim all our eager thought and keen-eyed penetration to investigate its origin, its growth, and its development, and ascertain the reasons that cause it to overshadow and render barren the otherwise bright spaces where the fairest flowers of loveliness should bloom, and the best fruits of sweetness ripen. One blemish would be sufficient, and perhaps more than enough, to excite our reflection; yet two sister faults, with their contrasts and family resemblances, invite our attention to-day; and a simile which offers itself, though very old, is not the less true, and applies with equal strength to both. Have

you ever—have you often—stood under the dark
canopy of some ancient cedar, my dear young
friends? If so, you surely have watched and
noticed how year after year the green sward has
failed, and gradually vanished under its branches,
and how utterly powerless rain and sunshine have
been to restore its freshness, because they could
not penetrate sufficiently through the impervious
dome of the towering tree. Or have you seen the
promise of the autumn unfulfilled on the sunny
orchard wall, because the growth of the neigh-
bouring elm, extending far and wide, absorbed
all the moisture of the soil, and left no nourishment for velvet peach or swelling plum?

Pride may indeed be compared to the cedar,
that towers grandly into the air, receiving floods
of light, and a crown of golden sunshine on its
head, yet casting shadows, cold and dark, around;
and vanity, like the elm, with its myriads of roots
and rootlets, has a close network of its own, with
millions of little meshes—a net into which it
collects and appropriates the thought, the care,
the attention, the consideration, which should be
given to worthier objects. Pride lifts its head
high, and carries it above the chequered paths of
the world, completely disregarding the joys and
the sorrows, the hopes and the fears, the struggles
and the rewards that may live and die at its feet.
It is haughty and disdainful while over-estimating

all human and terrestrial treasures, be they abilities, knowledge and talents, high birth, preeminence, or tangible possessions that may have fallen to its share; and yet how easy it seems to estimate all these at their proper value, to fix their confines and boundaries!

The outward signs by which pride makes itself known are forms and varieties of selfishness; its essence may be said to lie in egotism. The proud are apt to consider only themselves, and to look upon others as if they existed merely to minister to their wants, wishes, and expectations. Pride appears totally different from dignity, though the overweening fault often mistakes itself for the graceful quality, which consists in a sedulous avoidance of all that is otherwise than pure and noble in word and manner as well as in deed. "The proud at heart are an abomination in the eyes of the Lord," such is the teaching of Holy Writ; but it was said many centuries ago by one of the greatest secular authorities that to be proud is to wish to please oneself. This is a mere human lesson, yet it proves and explains to us the Divine censure of the egotistic fault. This self-centered and self-occupied desire, which is satisfied with its own approbation, and seeks no higher tribunal, must indeed appear despicable to omniscient Wisdom. Perhaps you may think, my dear children, that a fault, which seems to

isolate those who harbour it from the surrounding
world, and give them a certain kind of independence, cannot do much harm, cannot be a very
grievous failing.   It is, or may become, a great
one nevertheless.   Its often petrifying influence
on benevolence will not be denied.   The proud
heart cannot thrill very warmly for others; only
the power of sympathy, gentle, true and deep,
which means real, vivid, fellow-feeling, is able
to understand the hopes and the longings, the
despondency and the sufferings, the wants and
wishes of those who may need and crave our help
and our encouragement.

If pride often exhibits apparent indifference, or
even coldness, or, worse still, if it frequently wears
the garb of irritating superciliousness, this offensive bearing, this freezing manner must prove,
more or less, an impediment to much useful action
and beneficial influence, to much otherwise very
legitimate power for good, lessening, so to say, if
not destroying, the brightest happiness of the heart,
drying up the freshest and deepest sources of enjoyment, and dwarfing the real aim and true destiny
of life.   Vanity is, indeed, very different from
the sister fault.   It has been called love of approbation ; and, at first sight, nothing can be more
natural and more amiable than the wish to obtain
the favourable opinion of those by whom we live
surrounded, of those who may come within the

circle of our activity, who belong to or may be
drawn into our sphere of daily occupation, of one
and all who form our world, without distinction of
age, rank, or attainments. But vanity is not the
genuine and praiseworthy love of approbation.
It is an inordinate and extravagant desire to
please, to attract general and individual notice,
to excite constant and ever-increasing admiration, to shine perpetually, to be enthusiastically
praised and applauded, systematically flattered,
and worshipped among bewildering clouds and
almost intoxicating fumes of incense.

Among the ignorant and half educated, and
even among those who should be screened from
frivolous tastes by their accomplishments and
acquirements, vanity often signifies a slavish
adherence to externals, to mere baubles, to the
fancied importance of trifles; it signifies a constant
thought of outward appearance, of dress, of show
at home and abroad, and of the gew-gaws of
fashion. The emptiness of such pleasures, the folly
of wasting time in the pursuit of such objects, are
self-evident. Life is short, let us not play with
the earnestness of it, nor squander its precious
hours. Vanity has, indeed, many characteristics,
and gives rise to numerous faults. But more
countless than its distinguishing features, more
innumerable than its faults, are the misfortunes
which it produces. It is complete dependence upon

others, and not dependence for good service, for real, substantial, and useful gifts or boons, for such proofs of friendship, regard and devotion as please and delight both donor and recipient, but dependence for homage, for the excitement of applause, and for varied and ever-renewed panegyrics. Though vanity may always be hankering with insatiable greediness after such streams of honey, the world does not yield them incessantly. The supply ceases, ere long, and then the disappointment and irritation of baulked prospects become real torments; for vanity knows no self-esteem, no rational ambition, nothing save a mere hollow yearning for the smiles and blandishments of the world in the keeping and possession of the vainglorious. Within its domain nothing rests steadily upon its own strength and value, but on the appreciation of it by others ; all is superficial, mentally and morally, and often without any real misfortunes to darken their horizon, those who have given way to vanity become thoroughly and irretrievably miserable when the cravings of their weakness can no longer be fed and satisfied.

Pride and vanity are equally sensitive, equally irritable, because both are, so to say, the children, not of legitimate and judicious self-love and self-respect, but of withering egotism, and to both who are thus self-occupied, usefulness and devoted

service to the best interests of others become
matters of difficulty.   In other respects, the sister
faults stand very widely apart.   Pride concen-
trates all considerations upon itself, and, therefore, in its best, but, alas ! rarest development, it
may be compatible with strength of mind and
force of character, and while often disdaining
the opinion of the outward world, it may feel
strenuously anxious to satisfy its own high standard
of goodness, greatness, and excellence, while the
best development of vanity may lead to amiable and
loveable kindness.   Pride, however, often proves
hateful—namely, harsh and intolerant, unrelenting
and unforgiving—and vanity becomes despicable ;
the former a sin—the latter a weakness, the
compound of folly and inexperience, thoughtless-
ness and imprudence, incompetence and indis-
cretion, often leading to incalculable misfortunes.
But whatever the natural germs, the small begin-
nings of our faults and failings, we can always
hope to arrest their progress, to correct and
indeed to change them ; we need not despair of
curbing stubborn pride, and softening it into
that gentle and benevolent dignity, which delights
in faithfulness and in justice, in scrupulous
candour, in singleness of purpose, in undeviating
truth, and in the highest, most straightforward
integrity.   Nor need we abandon the hope of
transforming foolish and frivolous vanity into

constantly thoughtful consideration for others,
into love of approbation, not for ourselves, but
for the anxious deeds of glowing zeal, for the
good and successful works of our indefatigable
hands.

—————————

XX.

ON DUTY.

My dear children.

To the very young, who can know but little, either from reflection or from observation, whose thoughts are not matured, and whose wishes not defined, whose feelings are only half awakened, and likely to undergo throughout life incessant and numberless changes, to the youthfully ignorant, who cannot be said to have fixed principles, or deep and earnest convictions, and over whose path neither the light of experience, nor the brilliant torch of eagerly treasured knowledge can be said to shed illuminating rays,—the sacredness of duty is anxiously and perseveringly pointed out, so that the fulfilment of it may shine forth, and be recognised as the chief aim and object of life, as the best and truest and noblest achievement of virtue. Inclination, on the other hand, is seldom dwelt upon, for is it not sure to obtrude and assert its claims in mind and heart, and to crave a portion of the day for its indulgence and satisfaction? Indeed, it has sometimes been said, that one of the never-ending or ever-renewed battles in this world, is the conflict between duty and inclination—a conflict, which is supposed to have its seat in every breast, and to be modified only by strength or weakness of character, by mental or bodily organisation, by the rock-like firmness of staunch principles, or by that religious training, which is expected to resist all temptations. Surely that conflict ought not to exist; at least it should not be perpetually carried on. Is it not rather our task from the earliest years of thought and action to put an end to the dangerous and harassing warfare, and to reconcile duty and inclination? My dear children, let us do that which we know to be right and just, and we shall discover, ere long, that in reality the supposed antagonists may, and often do, help each other to reach the same end.

Yet how is the bright and happy perspective, the good in which all our efforts should culminate, to be attained? Shall we, in the exercise of all noble qualities, lend our ear to the soft and gently persuasive blandishments of inclination, or shall we listen only to the stern dictates of duty? Will the path, which we tread in obedience to well-defined obligations, however rugged and difficult it may appear, lead us inevitably to gardens of delight, where unfading flowers bloom in fragrant loveliness, where we may cull sweet and never-

deceptive fruit, and where crystal fountains yield
ever-flowing waters of refreshment to the weary
and the exhausted? Or will the sunny road, over
which the swift and bright wings of inclination
carry us with more than electric speed, conduct us
to the portals of the same paradise? Can inclination guide us to the fulfilment of our duties,
or will submission to their imperative behest
gradually coincide with inborn predilection, and
call forth every noble aim and effort?

My dear children, those who have given their
deepest thought, their most earnest and careful
consideration to the subject, have always deemed
it better and safer to act from a calm, clear, conscientious sense and conviction of duty than from
any impulse, however glowing and enthusiastic.
It is a better assistance to our conduct, and offers
far more certain guarantees of success. Sense of
duty rests on well-established convictions, on
moral and religious principles, and as they are
the happy result of earnest reflection, of accurate
knowledge, of pure and warm faith, they cannot
be otherwise than firm and unchangeable. The
sense of duty becomes so valuable to us in life,
because it is evolved from the most sterling part
of our nature, from the least fleeting and evanescent, from that portion of our being which,
humanly speaking, is not liable to mutation or
decay. It is the compass which helps us to steer

clear of the shoals and quicksands of even the
most stormy vicissitudes, whereas inclination
itself is more like a rudderless bark; it may, in
light and sunshine, glide placidly along, but how
often are not its white sails seized by the gale,
and torn rudely asunder! How frequently does it
not become the mere toy of pitiless tempests and
furious waves, to be swept by relentless seas and
shattered against the granite rocks of reality!
Inclination is subject to perpetual changes and
uncertainties ; it is unsteady and fitful, not to be
counted upon ; how can we trust it and give ourselves up to so wayward a leader ? It is unable to
guide itself, and is often swayed by alluring or
repelling chances, by trifles and bubbles light as
air and as uncontrollable; it selects that which
appears agreeable, and rejects what is painful ;
it is headstrong, self-opinionated, egotistic, and
therefore dangerous in the superlative degree.

It may also be deemed more meritorious, my
dear children, to hearken to the call of duty,
because in the balance of good and evil our actions
are supposed to acquire value in proportion to the
exertions which they have probably cost us, to
the powers of resistance and conquest which they
have called forth. And, no doubt, it is far easier
and pleasanter and more stimulating to choose
and select as a task one among many favourite
occupations, among many attractive pursuits, than

to overcome with persevering exertion and unruffled cheerfulness any obstacle which the sense
of duty may have placed in our way. The
former is chiefly pleasurable, and not incom-
patible with intellectual and moral weakness and
apathy; it does not seem to require any higher or
wider development of the mental and moral
faculties; whereas the accomplishment of all
labour, from a sense of duty, demands and
increases strength and energy, transforming zeal
and indefatigable activity—notwithstanding the
most severe exertions, struggles, and fatigues—
into real and inalienable treasures, into the best
and highest modes of training for mind and heart,
into the most perfect system of self-knowledge
and self-improvement.

To let our actions be carried out in ready
response to the unerring sense of duty is far
worthier of us as human beings than to permit
them to be merely the offspring of even good and
gentle inclinations. Our resolute will, guided by
earnest thought and true conscientiousness, should
be the law, the ruling spirit of our words and
deeds; our will, thus ably counselled, must doubtless cause us to work nobly and successfully in the
almost unlimited fields of action which surround
every wayfarer on earth. Inclination, on the
other hand, may be good and kindly, or worthless and even dangerous or sinful. Frequently

it is not aware of its origin, hardly knows its own strength or weakness, its own wish and aim. It reminds us of the wild weed, of the uncultivated fruit or flower in field or hedgerow.

It may be like the stinging nettle, or prickly thistle, occupying the space which would be far better filled by nourishing grasses; or it resembles the glowing bryony and the graceful night-shade, both attractive and yet poisonous; or it may be similar to thyme and marjoram and the bright blossoms of fresh clover, which yield fragrance and aromatic sweetness to the honeyed stores of the bee; and like these blooms and perfumes it may lend the graces of delight to the fulfilment of obligations, which unadorned might wound those whom we are anxious to favour and to serve. Or, like starry daisies, and blue-eyed violets, and the untended flowers of eglantine "blushing rosy-red," and imparting beauty and loveliness to otherwise hard and cold outlines, inclination may cause those duties to appear captivating to us, which would else seem only difficult and dreary.

It may strike us at first sight that we enjoy, not only greater inward satisfaction, but also greater inward freedom, when we follow the bent of our inclination than when we act from a mere sense of duty. But a closer scrutiny proves the contrary. Freedom can deserve its name and maintain its rights only when it acts in concert with

the dictates of religious and moral law. Chance
may be fortunate, it may fulfil our wishes; but
the absence of aim and purpose is the tomb of
freedom. Our reasoning powers and our conscience, the most admirably delicate, the most
exquisite and most wonderfully sensitive of all our
faculties, will point out to us the mission of
duty and its entire sphere, and in that vast circle
render choice and freedom of action possible, and
while establishing laws and rules, which must be
our immutable guides, they will remind us for
ever that inclination, unsupported by principle,
may lead us to the same goal, but that it might
just as easily lead us astray; for how often is
it not unexplained longing and yearning, an
unconquerable fancy roaming far and wide, or
a mere mischievous whim and bewildering caprice
—the playful child of imagination?

Yet, my dear young friends, do not forget
that to whatever means we resort, the fulfilment
of duty is and remains the chief object of our
existence. But the Almighty, in His infinite
goodness, has given us enjoyment as well. His
loving-kindness is so inexhaustible that the whole
earth has been filled by His paternal hands with
the sunshine of happiness. We walk in its light
and bask in its rays, we meet it and may win it
at every step of our pilgrimage, and strange and
difficult to believe as it probably is to the very

young and inexperienced, our duties, if steadfastly
persevered in, if looked upon as the great and
principal objects of our career, become transmuted into pleasures ; nay, more than that, they
do not merely assume and maintain the form of
the best and highest pleasures, of the purest and
most enduring happiness ; they tend to dwarf the
minor disappointments and annoyances which
occur in the road of life; they banish for ever
many of the most harassing feelings that can
possibly torture the human breast. Without
alluding to remorse, the rankling produce of
crime and sin, from the mere contemplation of
which we must devoutly pray to be for ever kept
aloof, there are self-reproaches which become
lacerating and festering thorns ; there is humiliating self-condemnation ; there is the oppressive
sense of uselessness by which the egotist must often
be assailed ; there is our own reprobation far more
galling and difficult to endure than the blame of
the world, which is certainly less severe, less constant, and being often quite unmerited, easier to
bear.

There is, my dear children, no swan's-down
pillow so soft and so unfailing to procure
peaceful rest as the consciousness of having done
our duty; there is no ermine mantle so warm
and comforting as the glow of our thankfulness
for having been graciously enabled to fulfil the

obligations of life. Let us therefore pray for
a continued blessing upon our efforts and labours,
so that, by the mercy of Almighty God, we may
be allowed to work zealously in the wide field of
human exertion, and reap those sheaves which
are our staff and our sustenance in this world,
and which fit and prepare us to enter the blissful
realms of eternity.

XXI.

THE QUALITIES OF OTHERS AND OUR OWN.

My dear children.

The portals of the most celebrated oracle of the ancient world bore the inscription : " Know thyself." The wise of those remote ages wished to indicate that self-knowledge is the source of our virtue and the secret of our future career, that it is impossible to know oneself, and not to derive real benefit from that anxiously and laboriously acquired lore; for is it not true that veils fine, bright and deluding—yet woven with extraordinary strength and tenacity—intervene between the keenest glances of self-scrutiny, and the tangled reality of our strength and our weakness, of our faults and our good qualities? And does it not require a vigilant search after truth, a most conscientious and indefatigable activity, to brush away the obscuring film that overlies our shortcomings, or the perhaps glittering gossamer that hides our failings, and that may even invest them with an attractive appearance? And, if we have succeeded in removing the screens which conceal the infirmities of our moral nature, if we have sounded the depths of our hopes and wishes, fears and doubts, must and do we not trace clearly for ourselves an undeviating line of conduct ? We should try, and we certainly endeavour to mark out, so far as lies in our power, a straight road for our journey through life, and that road would indeed be in itself smooth, easy, and light to travel upon, did we not encounter difficulties and obstacles innumerable in seeking to aid and serve, to please and conciliate, and, if possible, never to thwart our relatives, friends, and companions, or the mere fellow-pilgrims and wayfarers, whose defects and gifts, whose peculiarities of disposition, and whose circumstances, with their needs and advantages, their joys and sorrows, must and cannot do otherwise than exercise a powerful influence over our own progress, over our entire destiny.

It is one of the most marked features of our organisation that the moral and intellectual treasures and shortcomings of others interest us, and we may venture to say, claim our attention, not less vividly than our own failings and advantages. Surely both the duty of self-know-ledge, and the wish to know those around us, may and ought to become useful in the highest sense of the word, and we should earnestly try to make this combination conducive to the happiness of others, and to the development of our best qualities, which you are aware, my dear children, must secure our welfare and satisfaction.

It cannot be desirable for us to dive, so to say, merely into the recesses of our own mind, and to explore merely the cells of our own heart, thus taking no notice of, and ignoring completely the characters and dispositions of our neighbours. Mere self-contemplation, the habit of perceiving nothing but our abilities and acquirements, our shortcomings and defects, may lead to over-estimation and conceit, or to coldness and in-difference as regards the world, to indifference also with respect to our own faults, which appear dwarfed, and the danger of which is almost effaced in the mind's eye that sees and discerns no point of comparison. Nought but the attentive obser-vation of others gives us the true measure of our aptitudes. It teaches us a modest appreciation of our natural powers; it gives us a firm and clear consciousness of what we may hope to learn and cultivate, and shows us the limits and confines of our internal self. The careful and unprejudiced observation of those with whom we are brought into contact, shows us their wants and necessities, and thus it gives rise to that feeling of helpful pity, generous charity and devotion, which has been called the milk of human kindness. It leads us so far away and beyond the narrow boundaries

of self into never-ending vistas of brightness and
beauty, into never-failing harvest-lands of golden
deeds, into teeming vineyards, where the buds of
promise assuredly ripen into the richest fruits of
reward, that egotism becomes impossible, and is
replaced by every high and noble sentiment and
by every self-sacrificing aim.   For to know those
around us, is either to love, admire, and appreciate
them, and thus to gain much good from the
purest examples, or it is to know what we may
achieve by well and constantly sustained exertion
to make them better and happier.

Remember, my dear children, that without a
knowledge of others, true and profound, a clear
and accurate self-knowledge becomes an impossibility.   The world is the best, largest, most
faithful of mirrors, which points out to us unmistakeably and unerringly our shortcomings and
blemishes, and teaches us lessons, which the
greatest and wisest books often fail to inculcate.
The solitary anchorite, the world-renouncing
hermit, however pure and blameless his life, can
hardly know himself; it is only communion with
our neighbours which keeps alive the clear flame
of our highest aspirations. As to the cold egotist,
he never casts a glance over the unexplored
wastes of his selfishness ; he follows blindly and
unconsciously the bent of his own inclination, be
it good or bad; yet good it cannot remain very

long, as selfishness tends to warp and narrow all our views and feelings until they collapse and shrink, and speedily exclude every consideration, except one. If we recollect, my dear children, that each individual is but a link in the great circle of generations, and that, by isolating ourselves from the interests of mankind, we lose, so to say, or to express it more correctly, we almost sinfully relinquish our best and highest powers, those of usefulness, we shall feel the deep and unassailable wisdom of the old advice, which tells us to observe others attentively and dispassionately if we wish to know ourselves; and to look into the chambers of our own breast if we desire to obtain a correct and faithful knowledge of the nature of those around us.

The steadiest looks of observation with regard to the qualities and position of our fellow-workers, should not, however, make us indifferent to our own and cause us to pass over them without the most conscientious examination. Those who neglect themselves while paying unremitting attention to the words and deeds of others, or while restlessly observing and watching their attainments, their labours and rewards, must incur many risks; they forget to watch over their own improvement, they omit to develop their own gifts and talents, and to embrace the fittest opportunities of achieving

good and noble work in many fields of utility;
and, worse than all, they incur the terrible peril
of allowing envy and jealousy to usurp the place
of kindly feelings.   You are well aware, my
dear children, that such painful sentiments, unless
they become speedily extinct, must dry up the
fountain of all virtues, and poison all serenity of
mind, for they fill the heart with inordinate
longing, with bitterness, injustice, and ingrati-
tude, and thus destroy all internal happiness.

Remember, my young friends, that each of us
possesses in the cells of his heart and mind, the
germs of many good qualities, the development of
which may allow him to cherish the hope of real
excellence, to indulge in the bright perspective of
true and widely-extended usefulness; that each
and all may not only cull enjoyments and pure
delight   from   surrounding   circumstances,   but
that, under the protecting shield of Divine Providence, the activity of our hands and our
untiring devotion to the best and highest interests
may also gather gifts and treasures and blessings
for others.

A conscientious survey of the resources of our
inward being, cannot do otherwise than enhance
our contentment, for the Almighty, in His
infinite mercy, has indeed been lavishly and
inexpressibly bountiful to all His children.   Such
a survey of latent faculties and dormant powers

must lead to indefatigable industry and per-severance—to the growth and expansion of all good qualities, to the cultivation of all faculties, mental and moral and practical, to self-reliance and to pious gratitude. It is well known, my dear children, that in the world of the heart and of the mind, we see, or we may see constantly the same phenomena as in the outward world of nature. The untended eglantine of the hedge-row is bright and sweet, but how evanescent is her loveliness and fragrance; how much more beau-tiful, how infinitely brighter is her carefully trained sister! The wild vine hangs its graceful festoons over shrub and tree, but it is the culti-vated grape, which yields the cordial and the nectar. The diamond of the mine is a pebble dark and rough; when carefully polished it sparkles in the crown of kings. The pearl is imprisoned under the waves in rugged shell, unseen and valueless — but when adventurous men have rescued it from its prison by diving and plunging under the foaming waters, it becomes a precious gem. The stone of the quarry lies in the earth, unshaped, useless and inert, until transformed by the labour and art of man into palaces and temples, and proud cities, which defy centuries, and almost vanquish time. Marble is cold and silent until moulded and sculptured by human and perishable hands to immortalise and to transmit to the latest posterity wisdom, beauty, virtue, honor, glory, and genius. And if the kingdoms of earth and sea thus yield their most precious treasures, but yield them only to the most persevering and indefatigable efforts, why should not the kingdom of the soul, the seat, the birth-place of our highest and noblest faculties, yield great results, if strengthened by unflinching labour, and purified by ardently glowing zeal? Why should it not yield them, in their full and beneficent development, to our enjoyment of life?

Yes, active labour, by teaching us to be useful to others and to ourselves, teaches us to be happy —to seek our happiness, not amid the struggles of the world, not in the ever-fleeting views and chances and dissolving pictures of outward circumstances—not by comparing our elements of prosperity and well-being with those of others, and thus measuring and testing their worth by a fallacious standard, but by thankfully using and enjoying them—our gifts, talents, attainments and possessions, however modest they may appear. Vain, idle, and unprofitable are the exertions made to reach or surpass others in the race for gifts and treasures—be they intellectual or material—which we believe to constitute happiness. The All-wise and All-merciful has given to each of us a peculiar aptitude, the circle and sphere, where serenity and contentment may be sought and found.

Whatever our position, however humble and lowly, we may hope to win the boon and blessing for which we most naturally long, but we must search for it in the chambers of our own breast; and, like the insect which spins and winds the soft, fine, glittering thread, we must learn to evolve from ourselves the radiant halo, the happiness that is to surround us. Even if we could possess that which attracts and dazzles us so much among the possessions of others, be it gold and jewels, youth and beauty, talent and power, fame or genius, who knows whether the coveted treasures would bring us entire satisfaction? Would those gifts suit our peculiar nature and organisation? Probably with their train of duties and responsibilities, new and uncongenial to us, they would only fetter, or perhaps embarrass and disturb us. The child, in its longing after impossibilities, asks not merely for the jewelled rain-bow and the silver moon, but yearns also to shake off immediately its trammels, and taste the independence, and revel in the seeming freedom of a riper age: but how soon does that child, grown up to years of manhood, cast a longing look of sadness towards those gleeful days, so entirely free from harassing care and heart-rending anxiety? Strange as it may sound, there is not one human being, not the poorest and most wretched, who would willingly exchange

his lot and identity for that of any one on earth.
Some peculiarities, some circumstances, some
duties, even in the brightest, sunniest, most
gladsome life, would always repel us. We should
have to change every thing—friends and foes,
hopes, fears, and wishes, endeavours and expectations, joys and pastimes, feelings, inclinations,
thoughts, memories, and aspirations.

The knowledge that we could never calmly
contemplate or seriously wish for the strange and
incongruous picture of so undesirable an impossibility, should cause us to rest satisfied that our
share of duties, possessions and enjoyments, and
indeed all dispensations on earth as decreed by
our All-wise Father in heaven, are, and must ever
be, for the best. Therefore, my dear children,
let us endeavour to combine self-knowledge with
the knowledge of human nature around us, in
order that the former may imbue us with confidence and self-esteem, and the latter with the
heartfelt desire and anxious hope to follow all
good and great examples of generous kindliness
and devoted charity. Our confidence need do
no injury to that modesty, which ought always
to pervade our inmost being. It is our duty,
and should be our delight, to cultivate with
unremitting zeal every useful and noble germ of
talent, to foster it with active and energetic
perseverance, and when led to notice and admire

in others qualities and advantages, which it
would be well and wise to emulate—to strive
with all our might and energy, to win for
ourselves the same goodly attributes. Should we
succeed and rear and gather fruits of sweetness
and excellence, the success will not lead us to
vanity; should we fail in following where others
tread and cause roses to spring up round their
footsteps—the failure will not make us dissa-
tisfied with ourselves, nor envious of the more
fortunate and the more prosperous. We may
possess what our neighbour lacks, and our
neighbour may yield and achieve what we are
unable to offer. Let each contribute what he
can for the good of all; it may be small and
trifling, but the All-seeing will discern and not
disdain our offering, as it is laid in all humility
on the great altar of usefulness.

XXII.

MORNING AND EVENING.

My dear children.

At all hours of the day and at all times of our existence, we are swayed by the sense of our aims and duties, pervaded by hopes of enjoyment, by anticipations of success, by radiant vistas of the glad fulfilment of our wishes, and of the happy reward of our labours. Yet both our bright-winged hopes and the feeling of our responsibilities appear more vivid and more intense at certain periods of the day; they seem more clear and more defined, and still become subject to more changes and fluctuations; they imperatively claim and obtain undisputed precedence over every other sentiment, and then we bow often, as it were, unconsciously, to their powerful influence.

At early morn, for instance, the first emotion which fills our breast, is one of deep thankfulness. We have flung off the shackles of sleep, that fair and rosy twin-brother of pallid death, and we seem to revel in renewed strength. Body and mind, heart and soul, feel alike invigorated, and

hail with delight the revival of all their energies.
Then eager wishes and earnest intentions arise
spontaneously in the throbbing breast and in the
teeming brain. What are they, what can and
ought they to be? There is but one answer to
this question, my dear children.

We must and, I hope, we do anxiously yearn
to use the great gift of life, which has been mercifully renewed to us by the goodness of Almighty
God, after the torpor and suspension of all our
faculties, to use it in the service of the Lord,
and, protected and strengthened by His Divine
blessing, to develop the germs graciously implanted
in us, so that they may become good and sterling
qualities, and allow us to prove helpful to others,
to all, indeed, who fall within the ever-widening
circle of our duties and our exertions. And here
let me repeat once more, my dear children, that,
by endeavouring to assist others, to minister to
their happiness, we really establish our own. The
dawning day seems to lie stretched out before us
like an immeasurable field; it appears to challenge
all our powers of activity, and it deserves the zealous
exercise of them, for ought not each day to be an
epitome of life itself? Does this idea startle you,
my dear children? Are you fearful of the result?
Do you doubt your own perseverance and faculty
of labour and endurance? Do you feel alarmed
at the thought of difficulties and obstacles, afraid

of your own weakness, your own timidity? It is perhaps far better that the hardships and impediments in the way of your daily task should appear to you in such a light. By knowing them well, by looking at them steadfastly, you will very soon learn the strength required to vanquish their power; and in gaining self-confidence, you will acquire sufficient energy to conquer them entirely. Should you fail, even the want of success will not cast you down completely; it will not destroy your serenity; for happiness, strange as it may appear, depends far less upon success than upon conscientious exertion; the conviction of having struggled honestly and perseveringly with our own faults and with the disfavour of circumstances, raises us above mischances and disappointments, increases our courage, and pervades us with fresh hopes for the morrow.

But the Almighty, in His goodness, has allowed our opening eyes to feast upon the glories of nature, and one long, lingering look of admiration and thankfulness cast upon the earth as it wakes from its slumbers, must fill us with an overwhelming sensation of joy, with unspeakable feelings of delight and enchantment. What can be more marvellously beautiful than the rising sun, when it dispels the shadows of the night, and drives away with its glowing breath all the heavy mists of the earliest hour, chases them from mountain and valley, lake and stream, woodland,

and meadow, and draws asunder the black curtains which shroud the loveliness of nature! Slowly, gently, the enveloping veils fall to the ground, and disclose heaven and earth meeting in beauty and radiance, and then the whole creation becomes luminous, and seems to rejoice in its new-born light and life. The sun kindles brilliant fires on every hill and mountain crag, the distant peaks seem transformed into altars, and send up their bright flames in mute adoration of the Lord. From forest and bower, from pasture and corn-field, myriads of blithe songsters combine in jubilant chorus to hail the light, and pour forth hymns of gladness to the Divine Giver of all treasures, without whose will not one sparrow falls. Then the purest and brightest dewdrops sparkle in the sunshine, and provide their diamond goblets for the refreshment of every bird that flies, of every awakening bee that starts on its laborious travels; they bathe in beauty every grass-blade and leaflet, and prepare rare and glittering gems for the adornment of all the flowers of the earth. And how sweet is the incense which the expanding blooms exhale at early morn, which the cup of each lily and the heart of each rose waft through the realms of earth and air to the throne of our bountiful Father in heaven! But even among the works of man, in the large and crowded cities, the awakening day is felt as a great revival of the powers of nature and of humanity. Body and mind

feel animated and exhilarated for new labours,
new exertions, new endeavours, for the anxious
fulfilment of ever-fresh or ever-recurring tasks, and
also for the enjoyment of renewed pleasures, which
seem to grow up among the great obligations of
life, like the way-side flowers, the scarlet poppy
and the blue centaurea, that fringe and festoon
with their brightly-coloured bells and stars the
golden cornfields of the earth.

And now let us enter upon our daily labours,
my dear children, and work zealously and indefatigably, keeping our object steadily in view. Let
us pursue our aim carefully, with all our powers
of exertion, yet not selfishly; let each of us bear
in mind that the fruits of our labours are sweet
and precious only when they are reared and
gathered for the advantage and sustenance of
others as well as for our own.

Those who are still in the morning of life have
the easy task—though probably it seems difficult
to them—to learn, to study, to acquire knowledge,
to fit themselves for some career, business, profession, or perhaps art, which at a later period they
may exercise for the benefit of dear, and perhaps
aged parents, of younger brothers and sisters, who,
inexperienced, delicate or helpless, may require
aid, or for the maintenance of the home circle, of
wife and children. Sometimes both father and
mother become breadwinners; they must work in

order that the luxuries and refinements of life may
be added to the bare necessaries, and their endeavours, whether labours of compulsion or of love,
must be given to, and are claimed by wider circles.
Yes, labour is the law and rule of life; but be
heedful, my dear children, and let not vanity and
self-love be partners in your daily efforts, for they
have a baneful, a withering influence; they prevent the development of all good germs, and like
the blinding wind of the desert, which parches all
vegetation, all verdure, all freshness, they must
sooner or later dry up the stream of human kindness, and cause the heart to become entirely
barren.

But time is ever on the wing; gradually it
hushes the toil and moil of the day, and sweeps
with unflagging pinion both labourer and idler
from busy street and noisy market-place. We
return to our own roof, or lay down our work, or
we sally forth and stand on the threshhold of our
door. The sun sinks to rest in mantles of crimson
and gold; the approaching darkness glides myste-
riously over the outside world, and seems to
separate us from it, urging us to look into the
depths of our soul, into the crystal chambers of that
unerring conscience, which we cannot consult
too often, and to ask whether we have really
obeyed the voice of duty—of duty which involves
labours and difficulties without parallel. Have we

perhaps evaded or neglected it, or have we committed,
in defiance of its sacred call, of its warning voice,
any deed which our conscience would reprove? Have
we harboured, encouraged, or fostered thoughts
and feelings which we should shrink from and be
ashamed of avowing? Have we idled away hours
more precious than pearls and diamonds, or yielded
to irritating anger or passion? Have we spoken
words of harshness and scorn that hurt and sting,
or dealt wounds with lips steeped in guile? Or
have we endeavoured to give pleasure and to do
good, to forgive harm, evil, and offence, to banish
care and sorrow, to retain the affection of old
companions and win the regard of new friends?—
for the love of our fellow-beings is indeed one of
our great and bright and precious treasures. Have
we lost or won a day in the journey of life, and
how will it weigh at the time of judgment in the
balance of justice, in the balance of good and evil?

Self-examination so rigid and so truthful must
lead to humility; for, who can hope to answer all
these questions satisfactorily, and who does not feel
that, whatever has been accomplished, whatever
has been attempted, owes its success or its promise
of reward, not to our own feeble efforts, but to
the loving-kindness of the Lord, who leads our
steps, protects, upholds, and strengthens us through
all the mazes of life?

And with these feelings we fold our hands in

prayer, and look up towards heaven, and there we behold not one dazzling sun, but myriads of glittering stars, distant worlds, which seem to speak to us out of the immeasurable realms of space, and tell of the eternal love, of the infinite mercy, of the inexhaustible goodness of the Lord. In presence of these incomprehensible splendours shining down upon us from incalculable distance, we cannot but feel how small, how vain, how frivolous, how unworthy we are in all our aims but those which conscience points out and approves.· And then when the endeavours and struggles of the day have subsided, peace enters our breast, and gentle, yet fervent piety fills the heart, and, ere we close our eye-lids with the hopeful prayer that the morrowing day may bring us nearer to the fulfilment of duty, to the accomplishment of those obligations, which our own most eager, but unaided, endeavours could not compass, we devoutly say: "Into Thy hand I commit my spirit, when I lie down to sleep and when I awake."

XXIII.

THE BOUNDLESS GENEROSITY OF NATURE.

My dear children.

Let us try to realize the countlessly numerous and infinitely varied wants and needs of millions of human beings, whose requirements, moreover, seem to augment daily, and so to say a thousandfold, as civilization advances, and progress in arts and science, and knowledge and commerce and industry, extend their benefits far and wide over the whole surface of the globe, and appear to crave for those who follow in their wake, both more necessaries and more luxuries. Let us also consider that the earth in itself is always becoming more densely inhabited, and that, in some highly-favoured lands, the population is actually doubled in the course of ten short years. Surveying all these facts, we cannot be otherwise than astounded; for we know and feel, that through the blessing of Almighty God, bountiful nature satisfies all the children of the immense human family. Yes, nature, from her inexhaustible and ever-replenished stores, gives us

food and fuel, raiment and shelter. Yet, in
addition to the widely spread and always increas-
ing race of man, of those who live, and enjoy life,
or endure its pangs, of those who suffer and
struggle, and learn and work in town and country,
in village and city, who dive and delve in mine
and quarry, or dwell on the sea-shore or cross
the wide ocean, in addition to them all, nature
provides for far greater numbers, for incredible
myriads of animated beings in gardens and forests,
meadows and hedgerows, rivers and lakes, in the
fields of air above, in the waters of the deep
below. The birds of heaven, floating with the
breeze or soaring with the blast, the countless
tribes of fish, plunging into cool streams, the
lambkin frisking among the scented clover of the
pasture, the nimble goat climbing over rocky
ledges in search of food, the great collector of
treasures, the indefatigable bee, the ant, that
time-honoured pattern of industry, the brightly-
jewelled, inconstant butterfly, the insects, that
gleam like precious gems on the bosom of the
rose, the gauzy-winged flies buzzing in the sunshine, or skimming glassy pools, and the creatures
of every growth that cry and sing and chirp, and
mostly come forth when the light of day is fading
—the invisible, yet delightfully melodious nightingale, pouring out her plaintive ditties when the
busy hum is hushed, the shrill grass-hopper and

the monotonous cricket, the flitting bat, the
hooting owl, the leaping, splashing frog, the
moth rushing towards brilliancy and perdition,
the glow-worms lighting their tiny lamps on
fragrant banks—all these are fed and sustained
and strengthened by the rich abundance of
nature's excellent gifts.

And, in her boundless wealth and power and
luxuriance, nature provides, not only necessaries,
not merely that which is absolutely needed, but
with generous hands, she lavishly adds the charms
of beauty to her otherwise most precious boons.
Is not the earth most beautifully robed and
crowned and wreathed, her spreading mantle rich
with golden harvests, and purple vineyards, and
teeming orchards, and emerald meads, and bright
festoons of sweetest flowers? A ripening corn-
field is not only a promise of excellence, of the
chief and best nourishment vouchsafed to all
mankind—but also a picture of loveliness, as it
glows in the sun-light and waves in the breeze;
and each ear of wheat undulating so gracefully
under the breath of the west-wind proves how
plenteous, and indeed unmeasured, is the return
which every seed-corn dropped into the furrow
yields to the industry of man. There is not a
fruit that ripens, which, independently of its own
refreshing or strengthening qualities, has not
ever-varying charms for the eye, from the time

when the parent tree, fresh with young and
tender leaflets, unfolds its delicate blossoms, until
the early brightness, blown away by wind or time,
allows man and child, and bird and bee, to watch
the maturing of ruddy apple or velvet peach, to
watch the hard, pale fruit on the branch as it
turns into softness and sweetness, when warmed
by the sun, and touched by its glowing rays, it
gleams and glistens in ruby and amber and purple
brilliancy. And the carefully trained plants of
radiant gardens, or the wild buds and blossoms of
field and hedgerow, the fragrant herbs and
grasses, with their nourishing and medicinal pro-
perties, are they not beautiful and delightful as
well? attractive, though differently so at all seasons
of the year, holding out gifts and pleasures to old
and young, to rich and poor, to those whom
robust health enables to enjoy the whole world in
its wealth and grandeur, and to the sick, the
feeble, the languishing, who are cheered or
soothed by the sight of bountiful nature in her
loveliness, in her ever-renewed, and always beauteous garb; to the child that weaves daisy chains,
to the maiden that twines festal garlands, to the
aged, who adorn the perhaps dreary solitude of
their latest and darkest days, with the brightly
glowing roses which recall to them youth, and
love, and happiness.

Yes, nature is always beautiful, and bountiful

to all human and to all animated beings, and is indeed lavish of benefaction and of delight. The weary wanderer and the ever hungry school-boy gather the glistening fruit of the bramble from the way-side hedge, or the berries bright and wild and sweet, which enamel the soft green carpet of the forest; and for all the birds of heaven, grea and small, a perpetual banquet is spread on earth.

When the harvest is garnered and the gleaning is over, the hawthorn, so radiant in its snowy or crimson May attire, puts forth its tempting fruit, the prickly holly covers itself with glossy coral, the sombre yew shakes its tiny ruby bells to convene thrush and black-bird, robin and wren, to the great autumnal feast. Then blooms in splendour the scarlet poppy, or shines her pale sister; briony and nightshade hang their glittering necklaces and tassels on hedgerow and bower; they hold life and death, destruction and salvation in the same sheath, in the same cup, the soothing, healing, and sleep-giving juices, and the for ever quieting draught. At the approach of winter the ivy wraps its green mantle round the leafless branches of skeleton trees which shiver and shake in the wind, and flings its thousand protecting arms round crumbling walls and desolate ruins.

And the sun, which causes the productions of the earth to grow and bloom and ripen, for the

sustenance of all mankind, how gloriously beautiful it is, when tearing asunder the dark veils
of night, it rises over a sleep-bound and dew-
steeped world, and waking the winged songsters
in field, and wood, and croft, bids all zealous
workers cast off the fetters of slumber, and
bow down in humble adoration to Almighty
God, thanking His Divine goodness for the new
day vouchsafed to their labours! And again, how
marvellous, how splendid is the luminous orb, when
sinking to rest on a bed of golden clouds, it sends
parting rays to linger behind on the hill and in
the valley, chequering dusky, leafy paths with the
amber lights of its potent wand! And, in the
noon-day of its dazzling radiance does it not
brighten and embellish everything it touches?

And water, so necessary, indispensable, and
fertilising, so cleansing, so reviving and refreshing,
is it not beautiful as well as useful? beautifully
grand when rushing down in foam-white cascades
over rocks and boulders; beautiful when, forming
the mirror of the unruffled lake, it reflects the
deep sapphire of southern skies, or the steel-grey
expanse of more northern heavens; beautiful
again when the eye can scan its clearest depth in
laughing mountain stream, or looking from the
sea-shore, watch the dancing ripple of the waves,
or gaze appalled and yet spell-bound at the crested
billows roaring and surging mountain high.

So rich and inexhaustible is the renovating power of nature that the warring tumult of the elements cannot jeopardize its wealth, nor permanently prevent the accumulation of its productions and of its treasures,—not deluging rain, nor destructive hail-storm ; not drought, nor frost, nor the horrors of war and their devastations ; not earthquake, nor famine, nor pestilence. Nature recovers quickly from every blow, from every wound. Do not frequently the most overwhelming misfortunes lead to ulterior benefits and blessings ? The countries which have perhaps suffered most severely from an insufficient harvest, receive assistance from more prosperous lands ; similar calamities are more strenuously guarded against ; the quality of the soil is more conscientiously studied, the ground more deeply ploughed, more thoroughly drained, more perfectly irrigated, more richly fertilised, and the earth is made to yield more bountiful supplies. Commerce causes the produce of all climes to be carried by land and sea, to be bought and sold where most needed and most appreciated. Distant nations are thus brought into contact; they learn each others' wants and necessities, advantages and deficiencies ; and thus let us hope that the foundation of friendly feeling and brotherly love becomes established and cemented.

But, as a rule, each zone has its peculiar

treasures. Some countries possess corn, our daily bread, in richest overabundance, and some teem with vineyards and orchards, while others boast of gigantic woodlands, of firs and pines, and in the far west and east, of still rarer and finer trees, of spices, of silver and gold, of diamonds and precious gems, while under our steps extend those coal-beds, which were forests in eras long gone by, ere the foot of man trod this earth, but which are now pierced by mines wide and deep, and applied to innumerable uses. The seeking and obtaining, the fetching and carrying of all these treasures of nature cannot do otherwise than employ millions of strong arms and busy hands directed by energetic minds, and this work and labour should indeed tend to draw together, in amity and vital interests, all the nations of the earth.

But let us remember, my dear children, that, nevertheless, each section of the globe has received for its portion those gifts which its necessities seem to require most imperatively. Fur-coated animals inhabiting dense woods, and the fuel yielded by the ever-clad trees among which they dwell, appertain to colder regions. The warmer climes produce deliciously refreshing fruit and cooling beverages, and bark which heals and strengthens the weakened and the fevered frame. But we might go on incessantly, and still not

reach the limits of so inexhaustible a theme as
the productiveness of nature—on the surface of
the land, or in the bowels of the earth, in the
unexplored caves of the ocean, or in the transparent
fields of air.   In every kingdom created by the
all-powerful and ever-beneficent will of the Lord
there is the richest abundance of treasures and
of blessings.   The so-called luxuries, however,
sometimes described as superfluities, are comparatively rare, but all the necessaries of life are
plentiful.   The gleaming pearl dwells not in many
seas, gold is not found in every land, but corn is
yielded by the four quarters of the globe, water
flows from myriads of springs, salt is found everywhere, and there are few countries where iron,
the most useful of metals, does not underlie the
crust of the earth.   We cannot devote even one
short hour of earnest thought to the contemplation of the varied and infinite gifts of nature,
without adoring in humblest thankfulness the
wisdom, the mercy, the Divine providence of the
Almighty, by whose will they exist.

Yet, it need hardly be repeated, my dear
children, that, notwithstanding the lavish generosity of nature, man cannot live, without earning,
by assiduous labour, the precious boon of life. By
unflagging diligence the most necessary productions must be obtained, such as the bread we eat,
the clothing we wear, the dwelling that shelters

us. But this difficulty is a blessing; it keeps the entire human race in a state of robust activity and energetic exertion. In southern climes, where the soil appears to yield its treasures in spontaneous and unsolicited abundance, the inhabitants seem to have less strength and nerve than in colder, less fertile regions, where nought but daily toil and perseverance can win the produce of the land. Remember that there are endless varieties throughout the world, yet numberless resemblances and affinities, and that the equilibrium is never broken nor interrupted, for Divine wisdom rules tenderly and mercifully over the whole universe.

And while bountiful nature invites us to the cheerful enjoyment of her countless gifts, that same generosity exhorts us everywhere and always to ardent gratitude at the shrine of the Heavenly Father of all blessings. It preaches also indefatigable exertion that we may labour usefully and successfully; it exhorts us to eager and zealous search after knowledge in this magnificent world, which by the loving-kindness of the Lord we are permitted to inhabit, and where indeed there is a sermon in every stone. Especially, my dear children, let us take for our example the marvellous activity of nature. We cannot but follow with astonishment the perpetual transformations, the gradual, yet most extraordinary changes, the constant progress, from spring to

summer, from that glowing season to the cooler
autumn, and even to the apparently stern and
rigid winter, which is but the period of rest and
wholesome slumber when the snow covers and
warms with its wide ermine mantles the sleeping fields and pastures until they wake to a new
and still more teeming life, until they wake
to reward our diligent activity a thousandfold,
and to let their golden horn of plenty shower
down upon us even more than our well-earned
share of bounties.

But, my dear children, if the Almighty has
endowed nature with the richest abundance of
gifts and powers, if we can never cease to admire
His wondrous blessings throughout the visible
expanse of the universe, if sky and sea and earth
are full of His beneficence, how infinitely more
has not His Divine goodness done for us human
beings? Even the least brilliantly favoured has
latent germs and powers, which, if sedulously
cultivated, must yield the most valued fruits. I do
not speak of those splendid talents, which by the
Divine will and wisdom are not in the possession
of many, and, like diamonds and pearls—though
far more bright and precious—are comparatively
rare, but of those qualities which are to the heart
and soul what bread and water are to the body. Let
us, then, in imitation of bountiful nature, which
has thousands of fields of golden grain for the

nourishment of mankind, and myriads of crystal springs of refreshment for thirsting multitudes; yes, let us bestow the gifts of generosity and charity, of indulgence, forgiveness, and mercy, of devotedness, of patience, endurance and self-denial, and even of self-sacrifice, upon all who may require these offerings at our hands. And may we—still in imitation of nature, that holds out boons and blessings at all seasons, and never seems to grow weary of extending her generosity far and wide—may we be ever helpful, and never rest, never pause in our labours of love, or if we pause and rest—as nature seems to do in the cold winter time—let it be only when we do not see our way quite clearly, and appear to require tranquillity for thought and meditation, so that our future works may be more abundant and more perfect, and ever productive of better results. Nor ought we to forget that there is enchanting beauty in the productions of nature, and that we too should endeavour to embellish the works of our hands, of our minds, and of our hearts, so as to make them pleasing as well as acceptable in the eyes of others. Our indulgence should not humiliate but hold out gentle words of encouragement; our forgiveness ought to be tendered all wreathed with the soothing flowers of oblivion. Our charity should fold her softest, warmest cloak round the suffering or erring; our

mercy should be the purest stream of the sweet
milk of human kindness, our devotedness should
resemble the clinging ivy, our patience be like
the unfading, unchanging amaranth, our advice,
though clear and keen and well-defined, be soft
and gentle, even our rebuke should be administered,
not harshly, but with those looks and words of true
sympathy, which must win their way to the most
stubborn mind or irate breast; and as nature has
inexhaustible varieties of excellent gifts for every
changeful season, so ought our labours at all times
to adapt themselves to the ever-altering needs
around us, so ought the human heart to prove
inexhaustibly rich and generous in its gifts of love
and devotion to all who need them; and as "the
heavens declare the glory of God, and the firma-
ment showeth His handy work," and as "day
unto day uttereth speech, and night unto night
showeth knowledge," so should we, by the humble,
yet earnest, anxious, and zealous labours of our
hands show that we advance every day in the
knowledge of His Divine Power, and grow in our
ardently grateful adoration of His ineffable and
unceasing goodness.

XXIV.

DEATH AND IMMORTALITY.

My dear children.

INNATE and powerful as is the wish for change in the human mind, and gratified as that natural longing cannot fail to be even in the most uniform mode of existence, as no two days are ever entirely similar either in the circumstances that surround us, or in the thoughts, feelings and aims, hopes and fears which they suggest, there is yet one change, the greatest of all, from which it can be said with incontrovertible truth that all human beings shrink instinctively, whatever their position in the world, whatever their bodily or mental organisation. They shrink from it in sorrow and in happiness, in poverty and in abundance, in sickness and in health, in youth, in middle age, and even when infirmities seem to crowd around them. Upon this greatest and absolutely inevitable change we look as an enemy, to be perpetually kept at bay, to be banished to the furthest distance, but never to be entirely vanquished. The faintest symptom or the mere thought of his approach, fills us with inexpressible anguish and sorrow, and pervades our whole being with feelings of unutter-able dismay.

You need not be told, my dear children, who is the dreaded foe; for young as you are, his dark shadow may have crossed your path and spread his gloom around you. His name is Death, and it has been wisely ordained by Divine Providence, that almost every act of our physical existence should, as it were, tend to keep the dread fiend far aloof. Were it possible for us to court and woo death, or merely to contemplate it with perfect indifference, we should often be careless as to meat and drink, we should disregard shelter, fuel, and raiment, set the laws of health at defiance, face innumerable dangers, plunge heedlessly into perils, and live on in recklessness of all consequences, so far as our mere bodily existence is concerned. And, therefore, the salutary fear and the salutary hope are, so to say, constantly held before our eyes by an all-wise and all-merciful Goodness. I mean the fear of immediate or proximate death, and the hope of raising barriers of many years of health and strength between our certain doom and the ever-approaching enemy. Yet it is not only the attachment to life, its blessings, its joys and delights, which causes us to tremble in our heart of hearts at the bare prospect of looming death; it is the fear of the dreadful pangs, which must

precede the dissolution, the fear of inflicting
grievous trials upon others by the sight of our own
sufferings, of our own pain which cannot be suppressed or concealed; it is the fear of that long and
dim and mysterious separation from those we love
and to whom we cling in the warmth and depth
and tenderness of our affection; it is the fear of the
darkly-veiled unknown which helps us to live well,
which assists us perhaps to live usefully and
happily, to overcome dangerous temptations, to
accept quiet pleasures as a boon, and even privations as a necessity. And here let it be said, in reply
to possible objections, that as rules without exceptions hardly exist, there are some rare instances of
unfortunate beings who seek death, who wickedly
destroy themselves by poison, by plunging into a
watery grave, or by self-inflicted wounds; but
such acts of violence, which a diseased imagination
may suggest, are sad and sombre anomalies, and
do not invalidate the golden rule of man's love of
life. The coroner pronounces those insane who
lay violent hands upon themselves, and who sin so
fearfully as to cut the tangled thread of their own
existence. Some moralists who have lived long,
thought much, felt deeply, and sympathized truly
with the needs and sufferings of mankind, may
urge that to a few unfortunates—let us hope to
very few—the burden of life would be intolerably
heavy, did they not hope to be released from it on

the threshold of eternity; did they not look forward
to death with constant and anxious longing as a
happy and blessed deliverance. But such aberrations and irregularities need not be dwelt upon
any longer.

Life is the greatest of boons—a treasure quite
beyond price, which cannot be valued too highly.
It may not be rightly understood, and it is far too
often recklessly imperilled—but surely it is uni-
versally cherished; yet while we thus love and
prize it, the thought which every dawning day
should bring clearly before us, is the thought of
death, and of the many duties we have to fulfil
during each hour that takes us so rapidly and so
irretrievably towards the end; and with that array
of solemn obligations should arise the anxious
desire to accomplish them faithfully, and the
undelayed attempt to commence our work and to
labour uninterruptedly in the fields of life. And
as we thus act patiently and conscientiously, one
conviction ought to become firmly implanted in
our hearts, namely, that whenever death comes
near unto us, whether suddenly or after a long
illness, whether amidst sorrows and trials, or while
we are enjoying the highest bliss and the sunniest
happiness, when it draws nigh to our couch in
early childhood, in brightest youth, in manhood,
or in old age, it is mercifully sent as a heavenly
messenger of peace to save us from unknown

sufferings and perils, temptations and hardships.
Indeed, when we see it approach and stand before
us in our old age, we need hardly be told that
life is scarcely worth having when the loss of
many loved ones has made us sad and lonely, and
when, perhaps, innumerable personal infirmities
have deprived us of all pleasures, and thus weaned
us from the greatest sources of delight. All this
we see and know and feel to be irrefutable truth,
and though we witness the execution of many
death-warrants, which to our limited knowledge
must remain inscrutable decrees, we may well
believe that all are issued in bountiful mercy, that
no human being leaves this earthly scene too
soon, that none are allowed to depart whose
pilgrimage is not deemed to be accomplished.

And is there a power of divination that can tell
what futurity awaits us when we shall have crossed
the dark and mysterious chasm? Where is the
realm promised to God's children? What is it,
what are its joys and rewards, its lights that cast
no shadows; its days that know no nights; its
thornless roses; its flowers that never fade? No
eye, no lip, no pen can tell, not the most pious,
not the most clear-sighted, not the most eloquent
speaker, not the most erudite writer, not the most
profound thinker, and yet the belief in our
immortality is innate and indestructible. It is
our hope, our faith, our anchor and solace in

troubled times, our most radiant vista beyond
gloom and sorrow; and when all around is dark
and dreary, it lifts us far above the crushing
burdens of this earthly existence into spheres of
light and peace. Nor can this blessed belief be
annihilated; for have we not the knowledge of
our existence, the inborn certainty that in our
perishable body there lives an imperishable soul,
with conscience to point out the difference between
right and wrong, between good and evil? With
perfect truth conscience has been called more
than a glowing torch that nought can consume,
more than a brilliantly luminous flame which
never flickers, and no breath can annihilate ; for is
it not a speaking, a warning voice, a preventive
and a penal law : preventive, because it forbids,
and penal, because it punishes? It has been
characterised as more than an abstract law, as a
living, a just, and unerring one, neither too
lenient nor too severe, applied by a great internal
tribunal ; even more than that—it is the tribunal itself, notifying its verdict, its sentence of
condemnation to erring men ; it may become a
scourge, an invisible dagger, a slow and secret
poison ; but may it not also be a haven of rest, a
placid harbour of tranquillity for those who are
storm-tossed by the outward world, but who find
ineffable and undisturbed peace in the unruffled
expanse of its calm and clear depths ? And if

conscience, infallible conscience, gives us all
certainties, can it err when it points to immortality, when it proves that man, who was
created in the image of the Almighty, cannot die,
cannot perish, cannot be annihilated?

When nothing is destroyed, even on earth,
but all is marvellously transformed, when the
leaf-dust rises again into beauty in the blushes of
the young May rose, or the bloom of the autumnal
grape, surely we cannot be swept away from the
face of the globe to exist no more. The soul
must be immortal. We find the Divine promise
of its eternal life in many a page of the Sacred
Book. Reason and faith tell us of immortality,
and if any voice could be still more persuasive and
convincing, it would be that of the heart—of the
heart that has loved and suffered, that has lost
perhaps its dearest and brightest treasures, that
has been tortured almost beyond its powers of
endurance when relentless death tore from its
shrine and from all the encircling ties of a life-
long attachment, a brother or sister, a son or
daughter, wife or husband, father or mother, who
were adored, idolized, and almost worshipped.
Whoever has seen the angel of death touch with
icy fingers the warm lip and turn it cold, look
into the eye yet moist with the farewell tear
of sorrow, and petrify its last glimmering ray,
chill the soft grasp of the parting hand, and trans-

form it into hard clay ; whoever has witnessed these awful changes from life to death, must have felt nameless grief, torturing agony, and dumb affliction—not to be healed by any of the remedies of this earth—sufferings assuaged and comforted only by the strong and blessed faith that the dead will live again beyond the grave, by the undying hope of reunion with the loved ones, by the hope of bright and blissful immortality, which perhaps saved the sufferer from utter despair.

But, my dear children, there is yet another immortality of which we may be equally sure, and that is deathlessness in this world, among the scenes of our joys and cares, of our struggles, of our endeavours and success! You believe, perhaps, that in order to win eternity on earth, it is requisite to play a great part on the stage of the world, on the field of battle, on the high seas, or while encountering perils and planting the seeds of civilization in distant lands, to shine in the council chamber of kings, in the great arena of politics, in the calmer realms of art and science, while chronicling the events of history, writing beautiful truths, or still more fascinating fictions for the instruction and delight of contemporaries, and of hundreds of unborn generations. Thus, it is true, renown is earned, thus fame is won, thus talent and genius are crowned with undying laurel. This you know, my dear children, nor need you be told

that devoted men and women—call them saints
and martyrs—be they our brethren and sisters in
creed, or worshippers in a different form and way
of the same Almighty Father in heaven, philan-
thropists, benefactors of the human race in teeming
town and lonely country, in prison and hospital,
wherever there may be ignorance and poverty,
oppression, darkness, sin and sorrow, and vice, all
win glorious titles to the gratitude of millions of
fellow-beings, and live on in unfading brilliancy,
on canvas, in marble, and in bronze. But do not
think that the great, the powerful, the illustrious,
those heroes whose names remain emblazoned for
ever, and indelibly engraven on the page of history,
live on, while more ordinary beings who have not
laboured and shone in the broad light of the world,
are allowed to pass away without leaving a record
of their existence. They pass, it is true, but not
like mere shadows. Loving friends treasure fond
memories of the departed, but even these fade
and vanish ere long, and are buried incredibly
soon with those faithful hearts which harboured
and enshrined them; but though men and
women disappear in the fathomless ocean of
time, their good deeds are quite imperishable. In
the area of true benevolence and noble exertion
the name of the workman may be obliterated, but
the work remains more indestructible than stone
or iron; floods cannot wash over it, fires cannot

devour it. The more admirable the work, the more imitators will it call into existence, the wider will be its influence, the more lasting its effect. Nothing is lost ; a good example of anxious endeavours, of arduous labours, even of earnest attempts, lives on in ever-increasing fruitfulness and luxuriance, extending its silent and yet speaking power further and further. Though our name be unknown, though our perishable, outward form may lie concealed and forgotten under the green sward, and our initials be effaced from the slab that marked our resting-place, and that slab itself have crumbled away into dust, is not our immortality certain even in this world? Is not the double immortality worth living for, and should not its golden light rob sickness and death of their darkest shadows ?

In Memoriam.

SINCE the last words of this book were written, a great sorrow has fallen upon the heart of the writer. A heavenly blessing has been removed from her path, a source of constant joy and happiness has vanished from her existence, a loving daughter has been taken away from her side. She does not trust herself, nor can she wish to dwell upon her own affliction, but would like to place before her young readers—however faintly and inadequately—some record of the beautiful life which has so lately been extinguished in all its glow and sweetest loveliness. That life was so radiantly beautiful, because it contained in its brief but happy course the glad fulfilment of every duty. It was so perfectly serene, because it sought and found its own brightest happiness in giving pleasure to others, in ministering tenderly and joyously to the wants and needs of all who required help and care, in drying the tears of the sorrowful, in dispelling their anxiety, in banishing clouds and shadows from furrowed brows. Not that gloom and sadness had morbid attractions for the much-beloved. Far from it; though she felt so keenly and so deeply, she did not approach the sufferers with the anxious wish to share their sufferings, and thus lighten the burden of their woe, but with the earnest resolve to bid those who wept and feared and trembled, to weep no more, to fear no more, to look hopefully towards calmer and brighter times, to turn away from dark forebodings and harassing apprehensions, to remember that, in this world, however tangled and chequered its paths, there is, through the mercy of the Lord, far more sunlight than darkness, more warmth than cold, more felicity than misfortune, more joy than pain. She raised the courage of the desponding by the picture of the vigour and freshness of their youth, if they were young. Had they passed the meridian of life, she would point out, to lessen the pressure of their cares, the blessings still vouchsafed to them by Almighty God; and her own warm heart, full of sympathy for all around, was admirably formed to suggest a vivid appreciation of the best gifts and treasures of Divine Providence. Not satisfied with merely chasing away sombre clouds, she felt intense delight in bringing and diffusing joy and sunshine. When she appeared at the side of a dearly-beloved invalid, every sensation of pain and weariness and exhaustion seemed to vanish, every infirmity was forgotten. Her beaming face, her sunny smile, her laughter-loving voice smoothed the brow of care; her mirth, the constant flow of her high and happy spirits, seemed to diffuse an atmosphere of light and warmth, and to call forth all the smiles and ringing echoes of gladness. The devotion of her whole life was so enchanting, because it was utterly unconscious of its beauty and merit; it was so admirable, so complete, and so perfect, because it seemed to disappear behind the loving expression, the joyous manifestation of it, behind the assurance of its fulness, always tenderly delicate and gently bestowed, though never audibly given. It was unceasing, and yet it assumed every colour and tint. Its beneficent influence was experienced in the garb of loving-kindness and true generosity of thought and feeling, word and deed; it was evinced by un-bounded benevolence, by closely-veiled charity, by unlimited power of forgiveness, of faithful attach-ment and watchful affection, at all times ready and eager for numberless acts of abnegation, for days and years of self-denial. And to impart additional charms to that earnest devotion, she had a beaming joyousness all her own which caused her labours and offerings of love to become delightfully acceptable. Her sympathy was so true and deep and glowing, so quickly awakened,

and so abiding, that neither the happiness nor the
sorrow of others could ever leave her untouched
and unmoved. Divine Providence had indeed
been lavish of its blessings to her, and she possessed the most precious treasures of heart and
mind. All who had ever been brought within the
circle of her influence were sure to be received
into the deepest recesses of her kind, warm heart,
to be cared for and cherished there for ever. Her
judgment was so clear and excellent, her good
sense so admirable, her prudence and discretion
were so unwavering, that it seemed strange to find
in combination with so much serious thought and
earnestness of purpose, and with so much energetic
firmness, the almost child-like mirth and buoyancy
which never forsook her. Not only did near and
dear relatives, friends, and neighbours, with all
their hopes and fears, cares and struggles, trials
and joys, and the brethren whom we are taught
to love, and the little children, whom she drew so
irresistibly towards her, claim her warmest interest;
the whole visible world had indescribable attractions for her. Her enjoyment of the beauties and
wonders of creation was constant and intense. It
was the true and innate enthusiasm of happiness,
called forth by the marvellous works of God's
bounty. There was nothing in the heavenly vault
above, nothing on the green-sward beneath, which

did not exercise a fascinating spell over her imagination. The sunset, with its crimson lights and
lengthening shadows, or the early hours with their
rosy tints and sparkling dew-gems, the sailing
cloud, the silver veils of the moon, flung over the
slumbering face of the earth, the mysterious stars
keeping vigil on high, every bird, rising with
jubilant song into the fields of air, every blossom
and flower glowing and blooming in fragrance and
in freshness, every season with expanding buds
and leaflets, or waving corn-fields and ripening
fruit-clusters, with snow-wreath and with icicle,
held out alternating charms to her. With the
contemplation of all that is imperishably beautiful,
or ever-renewed in its loveliness, she embellished
her own mind, she brightened her own life. The
activity of that life was extraordinary and indescribable. It was so great because no selfish aim
or longing ever impeded its course, or craved
any portion of it. She did not crowd, but she
placed thoughtfully and carefully into it, not
merely the accomplishment of all duties, but
thousands of pleasures and joys for others, for all
ages and for all classes, for every hour of the day.
It was delightful to hear her dwell on the merits
and abilities of her friends, to hear her extol their
talents, their sweetness, or their brightness, unselfishly forgetting, nay, unconscious that it was

her own genial nature which had called forth the
exercise of the gifts and powers she took such vivid
pleasure in praising; unaware of the charm she
possessed over old and young, she was in reality
the sunbeam, which caused blossoms fair and fresh
to bud, and fruits of excellence to ripen. Though
her kindness was so constant and so great, so
gentle and so tender, it was equalled, if not surpassed, by the fearless sincerity that never shrank
from the most uncompromising expression of the
truth. She had, perhaps in the rarest degree, the
gift of candour, the power of frankness ; she felt
that she could lay bare every thought, every conviction of her mind, and need not fear lest she
should offend the most sensitive or wound the
most painfully delicate organisation. Every word
that fell from her lips was so honest and conscientious, prompted by a truthfulness so perfect,
that advice which often seems bitter, and reproof
which the most thoughtful can seldom divest of
the semblance of harshness, was welcome and
appeared delightful when breathed by her clear,
soft voice. All who listened to it felt that it came
from the warmest depths of a loving heart. It
never could hurt or pain the most susceptible, it
was an additional proof of sympathy, it soothed,
cheered, and encouraged.

As the whole surrounding world seemed to speak

to her with its innumerable voices, she collected from all realms of human interest the intelligence, the knowledge, the novelty that could not fail to attract attention. Nothing was too far removed to arrest her glance, to win her smile, or occupy her thought, nothing too small to awaken her sympathy. By the powerful charm of her all-embracing kindliness, she unconsciously transformed every trifle into a matter of real interest. She lived to serve and please all around her, to serve them lovingly and faithfully, without ostentation of goodness, to please them without weakness or vanity. Her life was a beautiful morning, all light and sunshine, warmth, and loveliness. It was a hymn of gratitude and gladness, sung on earth and wafted to the gates of heaven. To her sickness and sorrow remained unknown, for her the cold shadows of evening never came.

A trembling hand guided by a mother's sorrow-stricken heart will not have failed entirely in tracing the features of the much-beloved, if the young children who read these lines will keep in gentle remembrance the friend they have lost, and if they will strive to follow the example of ready self-denial and true benevolence which the writer has endeavoured to place before them.